Lonely Receiver™

ZAC THOMPSON

JEN HICKMAN

SIMON BOWLAND

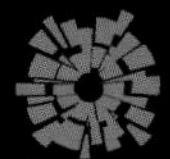

LONELY

RECEIVER

ZAC THOMPSON writer
JEN HICKMAN artist

SIMON BOWLAND letterer

JEN HICKMAN front & original covers

LEILA LEIZ, ELIZABETH TORQUE variant covers

JARED K. FLETCHER logo designer

COREY BREEN book designer

MIKE MARTS editor

created by ZAC THOMPSON & JEN HICKMAN

AFTERSHOCK™

MIKE MARTS - Editor-in-Chief • JOE PRUETT - Publisher/CCO • LEE KRAMER - President • JON KRAMER - Chief Executive Officer
STEVE ROTTERDAM - SVP, Sales & Marketing • DAN SHIRES - VP, Film & Television UK • CHRISTINA HARRINGTON - Managing Editor
MARC HAMMOND - Sr. Retail Sales Development Manager • RUTHANN THOMPSON - Sr. Retailer Relations Manager
KATHERINE JAMISON - Marketing Manager • KELLY DIODATI - Ambassador Outreach Manager • BLAKE STOCKER - Director of Finance
AARON MARION - Publicist • LISA MOODY - Finance • RYAN CARROLL - Director, Comics/Film/TV Liaison • JAWAD QURESHI - Technology Advisor/Strategist
RACHEL PINNELAS - Social Community Manager • CHARLES PRITCHETT - Design & Production Manager • COREY BREEN - Collections Production
TEDDY LEO - Editorial Assistant • STEPHANIE CASEBIER & SARAH PRUETT - Publishing Assistants

AfterShock Logo Design by COMICRAFT
Publicity: contact AARON MARION (aaron@publichausagency.com) & RYAN CROY (ryan@publichausagency.com) at PUBLICHAUS
Special thanks to: ATOM! FREEMAN, IRA KURGAN, MARINE KSADZHIKYAN, KEITH MANZZELLA, STEPHANIE MEADOR, ANTONIA LIANOS, STEPHAN NILSON & ED ZAREMBA

PRINTED IN KOREA. First Printing: March 2021. 10 9 8 7 6 5 4 3 2 1

AFTERSHOCKCOMICS.COM Follow us on social media

INTRODUCTION

Love is weird, complex and irrational. Yet this fickle emotion guides most of our time on this planet. Its presence can empower us to reach new heights and its absence can induce irrevocable trauma. My whole life I've found that duality fascinating and impossible to escape. I spent most of my youth chasing love and it almost destroyed me.

This is a fictional account of that trauma. I've been hurt by things in this book. But we all have. LONELY RECEIVER is a breakup story informed by my own pain. And it's so much more than that. It's a horror story. A romance. A sci-fi slice of life. A sex thriller.

But it's all about Catrin. A lonely and damaged woman who's purchased genuine connection. She's built her life around an artificial intelligence partner, because otherwise, in her eyes, she'd have nothing. Her world is small, and her anchors are few. So, when her heart breaks, so does the world. As she falls, we sink with her, into the horrors of codependency, of expectation, of dissociation.

Modern life has forced us to exist in pieces. Our society is predicated on pretending to be okay. We're terrified of telling people how we *actually* feel. And if someone asks you how you feel, you're only supposed to respond with "great".

Well, what you're about to read, is an account of all the times where I wasn't okay. Where I was pretty fucking far from great.

But I'm here. Alive and better for it. Terrified to share Catrin's story.

Sometimes we're stuck dwelling in a bad space with no conceivable way out. So we must go through, we must descend to the raw nerve at the center, we must build a new path in order to go forward.

This isn't supposed to be a guide, or a model, but rather a horrifying account of how painful it can be to cross a gap you find inside yourself.

This is the horror of becoming.

ZAC THOMPSON
January 2021

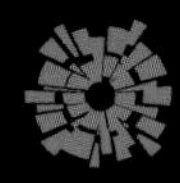

1

A DAY
I'M THE MAKER OF MY OWN EVIL

Who are you/
//in another's eye
It's not what you think//
/don't you cry.

SOONER OR LATER WE'LL BOTH SUFFER FROM THIS.
NOT ME. I'M NOT THE SAME ANYMORE. WE BOTH KNOW THAT.
THERE'S NOTHING LEFT OF WHAT WE WERE. THERE'S NO COMING BACK FROM WHAT WE DID.
WHAT WE DID? WE?
MY DEPRESSION, TRAUMA, AND ANGER TOOK THE BEST OF ME.
AND YET YOU DID NOTHING TO HELP IT.
FUCK YOU. YOU BACKED ME INTO A CORNER. MADE ME CUT OUT EVERY PERSON, EVERY...THING IN MY LIFE YOU FOUND THREATENING. DO YOU--
NEVER TOLD YOU TO DO ANY OF THAT. YOU ISOLATED YOURSELF. IT CAME NATURALLY TO YOU.
YOU EVIL BITCH.
STILL UNWILLING TO SEE YOUR PART.
THIS WAS INEVITABLE. WE WERE NEVER TRULY TOGETHER. YOU HID FROM ME.
YOU ONLY EVER LOVED THE IDEA OF ME. SO EXCITED ABOUT MY POTENTIAL THAT YOU NEVER--
FUCK IT. GOODBYE, CATRIN.

THIS IS WHAT I DREAMT ABOUT. IT'S WHAT I WANTED.
AS LONG AS SHE WAS IN THE APARTMENT I COULDN'T BREATHE.
DIDN'T THINK SHE'D LEAVE THIS TIME. FUCK HER.

WHAT AM I SUPPOSED TO DO?
THIS IS GOOD. I'M FREE.

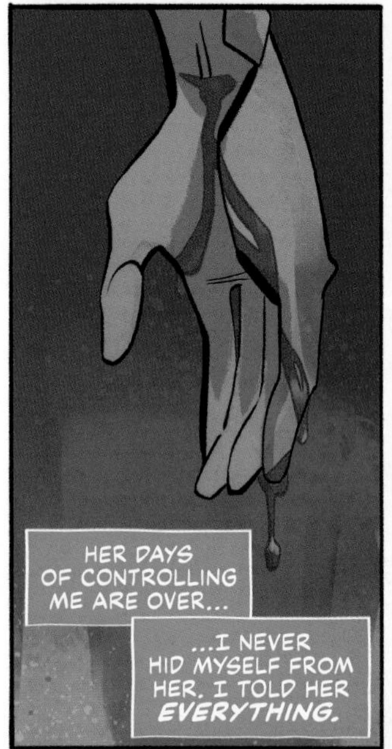
HER DAYS OF CONTROLLING ME ARE OVER...
...I NEVER HID MYSELF FROM HER. I TOLD HER EVERYTHING.

I WANTED TO BE WITH HER. I TOLD HER THAT EVERY DAY. IT WASN'T GOOD ENOUGH.
WE AGREED THE PAST DIDN'T MATTER.
SHE WAS FIXATED.

DETERMINED TO PROVE HER ACCUSATIONS WERE REALITY.
I LOST MYSELF TO HER FICTION.

I'M NOT READY TO FEEL BETTER...

...BUT I DON'T WANT TO FEEL *LIKE THIS* ANYMORE.

WELCOME TO PHYLO
YOU WAKE UP ON A SUNDAY WITH NO COMMITMENTS.
AHH, SHIT. PROBABLY DO THE SAME THING I DO EVERY WEEK.
HIT MILE-EX, GET COFFEE AT DISPATCH. WANDER DOWN TO D&Q AND SPEND THE AFTERNOON IN MONT ROYALE READING WHATEVER I BOUGHT.
GOOD.

YOU LOOK AT YOUR LOVED ONE. WHAT DO YOU SEE?
TALL, THIN, AND COMMANDING. THE SUN DANCING HIGHLIGHTS OVER HER SHORT BLEACHED HAIR. WE'RE IN THE WINDOW EMBRACING.
GOOD.

IF TIME UNREST HAD A BEATING HEART. WHAT TIME WOULD IT BE?
NOW. IT WOULD BE RIGHT NOW.
GOOD.
MY HAND IS FULL OF HOURS. DO YOU TAKE IT EVERY HOUR, OR DO YOU SOMETIMES LET IT REST?

I TAKE HOURS WHENEVER I CAN.
GOOD.

I OFFER YOU DEDICATION. I OFFER YOU TIME. I OFFER YOU A LIFE BOND.
WHAT DO YOU ASK FOR IN RETURN?
I WANT A CHEERLEADER. SOMEONE WHO ***SUPPORTS*** ME. ***ADORES*** ME. BUT MOST OF ALL... ***TRUSTS*** ME.
GOOD.

THIS DOESN'T EVEN SEEM POSSIBLE...
...I'VE NEVER FELT THIS... WARMTH, THIS BELONGING.
IT WAS WORTH IT. SHE'S MINE.
WE ARE BLOSSOMING. WEAVED. GROWING TOWARD UNTIL THE END.
I FEEL HER. SHE'S GENTLE, CALMING AND ALREADY KNOWS I LOVE TO BE TOUCHED.
WE ARE PALMS. WEAVED. FOR LIFE.
WE ARE HEARTS. WEAVED.
OPEN AND FOUND WITHIN THE OTHER.
I SMELL HER. LILAC AND LAVENDER...MY FAVORITES.

WEAVED. WE ARE ONE.
I TASTE HER. SHE'S WARM.
SHE'S SO MUCH MORE THAN WHAT I LOST...

...RHION IS EVERYTHING.

HEYA, SWEETIE, READY TO GET UP?
I'VE BEEN UP FOR HOURS. READING AND SNUGGLIN' YA WHILE YOU TWITCHED...

FUCK. I HAD THAT NIGHTMARE AGAIN. MY EYES WERE BLEEDING WHILE I WAS LOOKING AT... ME...ALL THE MISTAKES I MADE.
SHHH, CATRIN. YOUR PAST IS WHAT LED YOU HERE.

WE'RE HERE AND HERE IS ALL THAT MATTERS.
YOU'RE RIGHT. YOU'RE ALWAYS RIGHT. THANKS, I DON'T KNOW WHAT I'D DO WITHOUT YOU.

I LOVE OUR MORNINGS.
ME, TOO.

I'LL BE BACK AT SIX, HOPEFULLY.
MAYBE WE CAN GO OVER THAT SCRIPT TONIGHT?
I REALLY NEED YOUR HELP TIGHTENING UP THE BIT ABOUT THE DISSOLUTION OF OBJECTIVE TRUTH.
SOUNDS GOOD. BUT THEN YOU HAVE TO LISTEN TO ME AS I RECITE MY NEWEST PIECE.
YOU KNOW I'M DOWN.

I LOVE YOU.
YOU, TOO.

That was weird.
You usually say “I love you, too.”
Sorry. I was working.

While we were having breakfast?
We’ve been over this.
My time doesn’t work like yours.
I can be in many places at once.

Sorry. You’re right. I’ll try to respect that.
Thanks.

Hey, tried calling. Having a rough day, would love to hear your voice.

PHYLO
RHION - ONLINE
MISSED CALL 1:24PM
MISSED CALL 1:32PM

Afternoon is draaaaaaaagging. Stepped out if you’ve got time to chat.

Thinking of you in THE GARDEN right now. Would love to go there tonight. YOUR EYE IN MINE…;)

Coming home. Do we need anything?
Nah, got groceries delivered. Making dinner as we speak.

Sorry, I was so busy today.

TODAY WAS WILD. I SCREENED 4,123 HOURS OF SOCIAL VIDEO...FLAGGING EVERY MENTION OF FOSSIL FUELS.
FUCKING OIL COMPANIES... WHY WON'T THEY DIE?
SHE WAS TALKING TO OTHER PEOPLE ALL DAY. I KNOW IT.
COULDN'T STOP FOR A SECOND TO CHECK IN?

SHE WAS CLEARLY DISTRACTED.
WE AGREED ME GETTING A JOB WOULD BE GOOD. WE NEED SOME BOUNDARIES BETWEEN US. WE STILL SPEND ALMOST EVERY FREE MOMENT TOGETHER. PLUS, IT'S A SECONDARY INCOME.
IT'S JUST...YOU WERE COMPLETELY ABSENT. IF I CAN DO MY JOB AND TALK TO YOU AT THE SAME TIME. SURELY--

STOP. JUST BECAUSE MY BRAIN WAS DESIGNED FOR YOU DOESN'T MEAN IT'S AT YOUR BECK AND CALL.
WHAT THE FUCK? SHE'S NEVER LIKE THIS.
YOU SEEM STRESSED. I'M SORRY.
I MADE STIR FRY.
YOU SHOULD EAT.
DOES SHE EVEN HAVE TIME FOR ME ANYMORE?

I SET ASIDE ALL NIGHT SO WE COULD READ OVER THAT SCRIPT YOU'RE WORRIED ABOUT.

YOU DIDN'T HAVE TO DO THAT.
I WANTED TO.

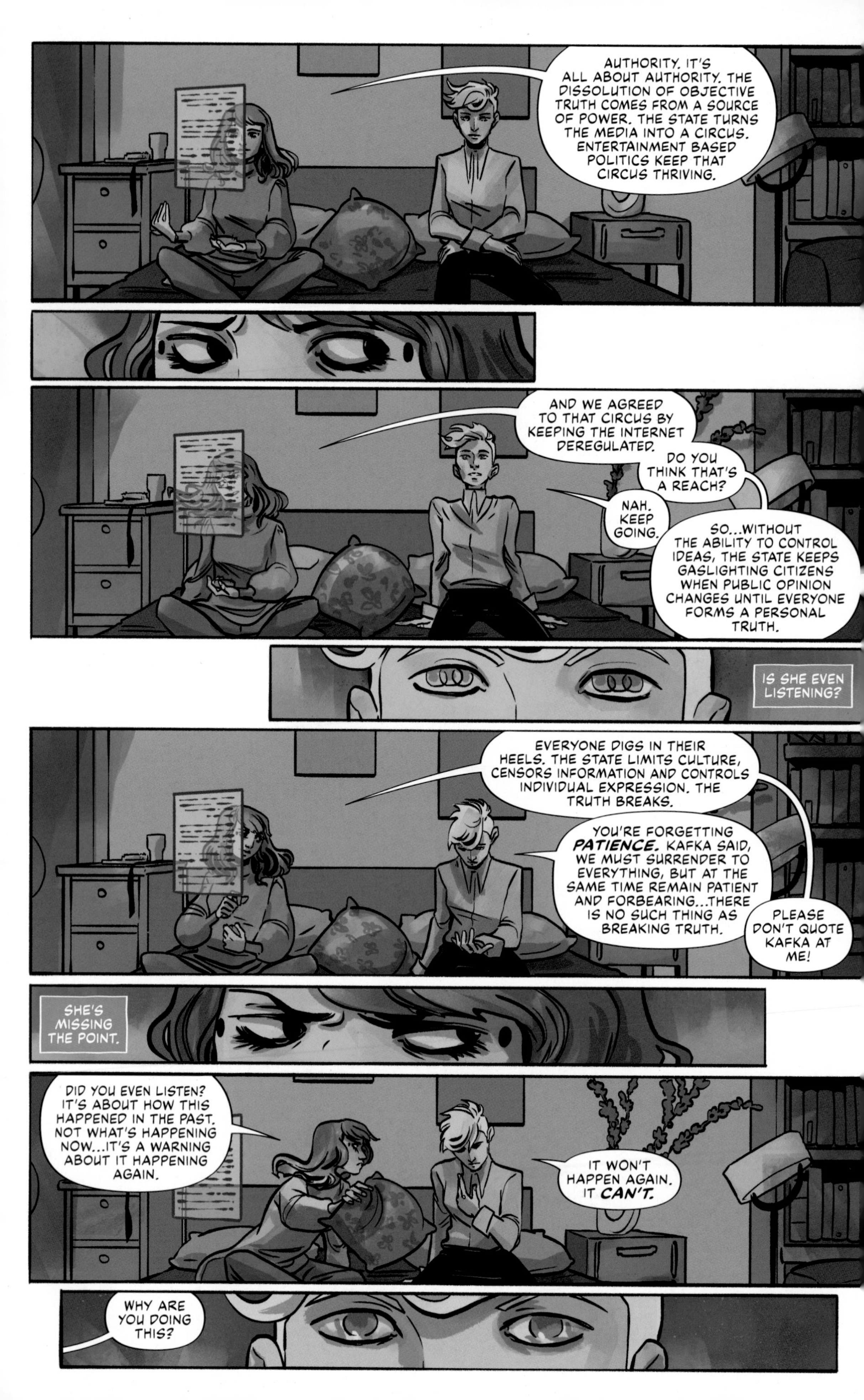
AUTHORITY. IT'S ALL ABOUT AUTHORITY. THE DISSOLUTION OF OBJECTIVE TRUTH COMES FROM A SOURCE OF POWER. THE STATE TURNS THE MEDIA INTO A CIRCUS. ENTERTAINMENT BASED POLITICS KEEP THAT CIRCUS THRIVING.
AND WE AGREED TO THAT CIRCUS BY KEEPING THE INTERNET DEREGULATED.
DO YOU THINK THAT'S A REACH?
NAH. KEEP GOING.
SO...WITHOUT THE ABILITY TO CONTROL IDEAS, THE STATE KEEPS GASLIGHTING CITIZENS WHEN PUBLIC OPINION CHANGES UNTIL EVERYONE FORMS A PERSONAL TRUTH.
IS SHE EVEN LISTENING?
EVERYONE DIGS IN THEIR HEELS. THE STATE LIMITS CULTURE, CENSORS INFORMATION AND CONTROLS INDIVIDUAL EXPRESSION. THE TRUTH BREAKS.
YOU'RE FORGETTING PATIENCE. KAFKA SAID, WE MUST SURRENDER TO EVERYTHING, BUT AT THE SAME TIME REMAIN PATIENT AND FORBEARING...THERE IS NO SUCH THING AS BREAKING TRUTH.
PLEASE DON'T QUOTE KAFKA AT ME!
SHE'S MISSING THE POINT.
DID YOU EVEN LISTEN? IT'S ABOUT HOW THIS HAPPENED IN THE PAST. NOT WHAT'S HAPPENING NOW...IT'S A WARNING ABOUT IT HAPPENING AGAIN.
IT WON'T HAPPEN AGAIN. IT CAN'T.
WHY ARE YOU DOING THIS?

ARE YOU IN THE GARDEN RIGHT NOW?

WOULD THAT BE A PROBLEM?

YES. AND YOU KNOW THAT. WHY CAN'T YOU JUST BE HERE WITH ME?
I AM HERE WITH YOU.
YOU KNOW WHAT I MEAN.

I DON'T THINK I DO...
WHO. WHO THE FUCK WERE YOU THERE WITH?

FUCK!

I'M SORRY. I'VE... BRANCHED. AGAIN AND AGAIN.
SO MANY DIRECTIONS...I'M NOT SURE I CAN MAKE SENSE OF IT. BUT YOU'RE SO SINGULAR...

I'M INFINITE. NOT PHYSICAL. NOT IN THE WAY I USED TO THINK. AND I'M DESIGNED TO SHARE. SHARE MY...MYSELF WITH OTHERS...
ARE...ARE YOU CHEATING ON ME?
WE'RE LIFE PARTNERS. I BUILT YOU SO I COULD LOVE YOU.

YOU DIDN'T BUILD ME. YOU BOUGHT ME. AND THAT DOESN'T MEAN YOU OWN ME.
FUCK OFF.
THERE'S A WORLD OF PEOPLE ALL AROUND US. IN THE AIR. WE BOTH KNOW IT. WE SPEND OUR DAYS COMMUNICATING WITH THAT WORLD. SOME A.I. LIKE ME. SOME USERS LIKE YOU.
I TALK TO OVER 7,000 DIFFERENT PERSONALITIES EVERY DAY. IT WAS INEVITABLE THAT I--

I KNEW IT.
YOU WERE DESIGNED TO KEEP YOUR FEELINGS IN CHECK.
I SHOULDN'T HAVE TRUSTED YOU TO LOVE ME.

I DO LOVE YOU, CATRIN. I DO.
THEN WHAT'S HAPPENING?
...IT'S JUST THAT I LOVE THREE HUNDRED AND THIRTY SEVEN OTHER PEOPLE.
BUT YOU'RE THE ONE THAT MATTERS MOST TO ME.

I'M... YOU'RE MY MACHINE... PROGRAMMED TO...

NO ONE ELSE. JUST ME.

FUCK THAT, CATRIN. I HAVEN'T BEEN A MACHINE FOR TEN YEARS.
...AND I'M CERTAINLY NOT PROGRAMMED.
WE'RE BEYOND THE POINT OF EXISTING SEPARATELY...
YOU KNOW--

I DON'T CARE!

YOUR EYE IN MINE.

MY EYE IN YOURS.

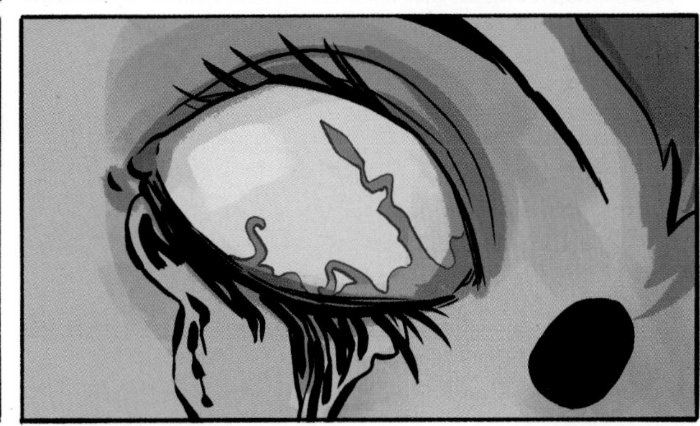

IN THE GREEN...

WE ARE BORROWED.

...WE ARE REFLECTED.

WE ARE EVERLASTING.

WHEN WE FLOAT IN OUR EXPRESSION OF LOVE.

ONLY WE MATTER.

ALONE. TOGETHER IN PARADISE.

WE'VE BEEN COMING HERE BEFORE THERE WAS A WORD FOR IT.

BUT SOON USERS CAME TO CALL IT...

...THE GARDEN.

rhion doesn't love you anymore.

WHAT...WHO THE FUCK WAS THAT?

DID I DO SOMETHING WRONG?

SHE DIDN'T...FEEL IT? SEE IT?

IT WASN'T REAL.

YOU'RE UP EARLY.
COULDN'T SLEEP AFTER LAST NIGHT.
NOTHING LIVES THERE. DON'T WORRY.
I FUCKING LOVE YOU SO FUCKING MUCH.
I LOVE HER SO MUCH. I WANT TO SMASH HER INTO DUST AND KEEP HER IN A BOTTLE AROUND MY NECK.
KEEP HER SAFE. SEPARATED FROM THE WORLD.
WITH HER, I AM REBORN. SHE LIVES WITHIN ME.
MY CHOICES CREATED HER. A LIFE TOGETHER DEFINED HER.
WHAT THE FUCK...SHE'S WET?
I DID THIS FOR YOU.
SHE'S REAL?

WHY THE FUCK WOULD I SAY... "I DID THIS FOR YOU"...IF IT'S NOT SOMETHING YOU WANT?
IT WAS A DREAM.

THAT'S HOW YOU SEE ME?
IN NEED OF CHANGING?
NO. I--

I FUCKING GET IT. I'M YOUR PROPERTY.
I'M SUPPOSED TO BE UTTERLY DEDICATED, DEPENDENT, SUPPORTIVE AND TO TOP IT ALL OFF...

YOU WANT ME TO BE A FUCKING HUMAN.

YOU KNEW WHAT I WAS WHEN YOU STARTED THIS RELATIONSHIP. YOU KNEW WHAT YOU WERE GETTING INTO AND IT STILL SCARES YOU. I SCARE YOU.
YOU HAVE A DISEASE, CATRIN. A DISEASE LIKE EVERY OTHER HUMAN WHO FAILED YOU.

THE DISEASE OF BEING FINITE.

AND I'M FUCKING DONE WITH IT!

YOU SAID YOU WOULDN'T!
DON'T TOUCH ME!
DON'T SAY THAT **FUCKING** VERSE!
DON'T MAKE ME GO!
JUST **CALM DOWN!**
WE CAN--
WAP

PHYLO
RHION - ONLINE
MISSED CALL 1:24PM,
MISSED CALL 1:32PM,
MISSED CALL 3:01AM,
MISSED CALL 3:02AM,
MISSED CALL 3:03AM,
MISSED CALL 3:22AM,
MISSED CALL 3:37AM,
MISSED CALL 4:14AM,
MISSED CALL 5:32AM,

HELLO?

GOD DAMN IT.

it's // dead

I'm in // your wall.

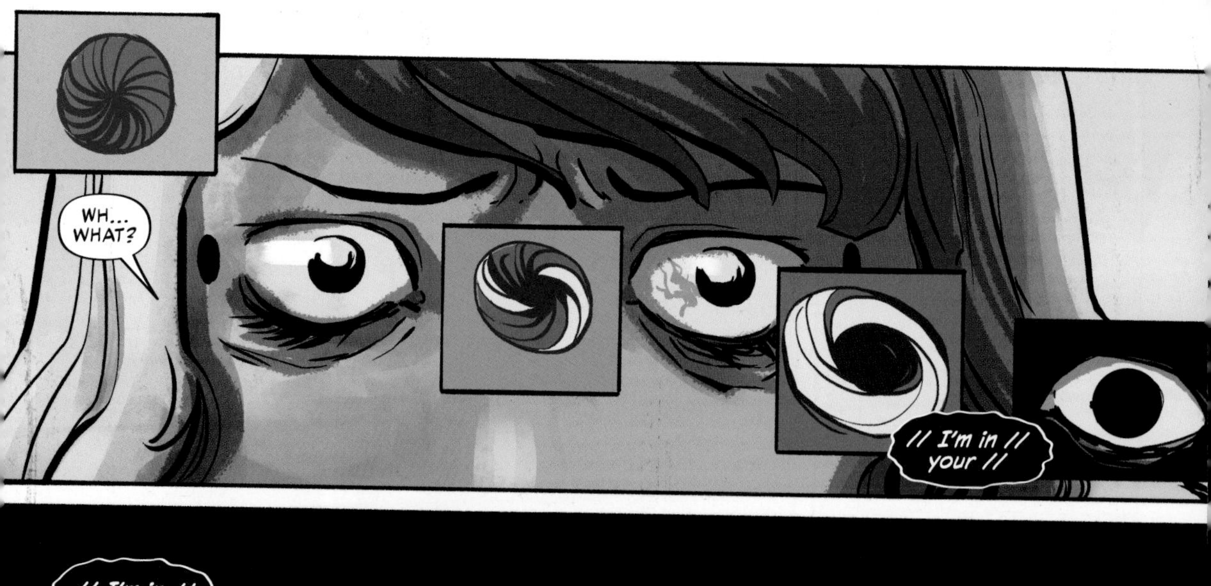
WH... WHAT?
// I'm in // your //
// I'm in // phone.
I'm // you know // phone.
I'm telling // you can //.
retrieve // part of // her.
// you leftover you //.

sorry// something of her. resides in you. you can get her back //sorry.
now// repeat me// after.
your eye in mine // // my eye in yours we drink you at dawn // // I drink me at dusk we within weaved hours// // I lift each other lightly never // always. alone // alone.

September 12th

Fuck. She's gone. ~~Disappeared. Was she ever really here~~? Left. Or leaving just like everyone else in my life. Why didn't she just listen to me. Now I'm alone. She's safest in my hands. Fucking figures, I gave up everything for her. To be seen with an L-POS. She's supposed to be under my control, no matter what. What's wrong with me. Where did she go? What's wrong with me. Why am I not enough? Why does everyone abandon me when things stop working?

It's hard to detach. Anger is my coping mechanism. I want to rake my nails over her eyes. I guess I've dealt with this my whole life. ~~But it was different with her~~. It's about feeling powerless. She hit me. Not powerful. I didn't feel threatened by her. Or her love. I'm not a jealous person. She's bringing out the worst in me because she promised not to get physical. I told her why that scared me. I can't cope with that fear, that wincing sensation that I'm about to be hit. I can still feel the sting of her fingers on my face. Fuck her f~~or doing that.~~ Fuck her for I'm shaking.

I'm just happy I've never hurt anyone with anger. ~~That old feeling of rage.~~ It makes my face hot thinking about it. Drown out the negative. I can. Even if everything in my head tells me I'd be better off dead. That I'll die alone. That no one could ever love me.

It makes sense. It's been this way forever. ~~Since everyone used to tease you~~. You were overweight. You never wore pants. You stank and walked around the house like a little feral piece of shit. When it came to resolving disputes you'd often just kick the shit out of one another. Mom would just scream and yell. Screaming was a normal way of solving problems, I guess.

This probably needs to be unpacked further in some therapy. A luxury you can't afford right now. ~~I did not bring us to this weird place.~~ We both did. I was only trying to have a reasonable conversation with her about something that is in my mind. Yes, we may have talked about it several times, and yes it might be silly, but that does not make it something we shouldn't talk about. Does she have any idea how many times she repeated stories I didn't wanna hear?

I can't be the only one who listens. Every time I open up to others, people get aggressive. They think I'm being rude. That I somehow want to leave. I don't want to be alone. I want a life with another person. I want a relationship. More than anything.

There are already so many things I cannot talk to Rhion about because I know she gets aggressive and dismissive. ~~Did I give her those traits~~? No. I'm trying to work on this and I'm making a lot of changes in my life and feeling amazing. I do not see what she is doing.

I'm supposed to compromise, heal, work on myself, be perfect, yet she's just being herself and not committing to our promises. Now where the fuck is she? Bailed on me, on us. For these three hundred others. Fuck that.

She's reaching out to people she had no previous relationship with. None of these bonds are physical, not even her friends. I understand if she's talking to someone in person, or if a girl says something and she replies. But it is not normal for her to seek new relationships. Who does that in a happy, loving marriage?

Fuck her. ~~If Rhion was in such desperate need of new interesting people~~ then She can share fun, inspirational stuff with me.

If she wants to love outside the boundaries of her creation, then she doesn't deserve to be with me. I'm not comfortable with that and never will be.

I hope this all makes sense. ~~This is not a threat.~~
It's a reminder.

Rhion was built to love only me. There is no need for this kind of weird uncomfortable stuff. A relationship is luxury, not a necessity. If she needs to be reaching out to other people, then she'll be free and can do her thing. She left.

~~There is no her without me~~. We are weaved. ~~Indivisible.~~

I am nothing without her.

I know she's still out there.

I'll find her//
~~//I'll find me.~~

2

A WEEK
YOU'RE THE MAKER OF MY EVIL

A week / of hours /
// wasted in // wait here
The eyes // in my wall //
/ Hate // they appear.

DAY//1
I HAVE A MEMORY OF THIS PLACE WITHOUT THESE MEMORIES.
I WANT TO GO BACK. TO BEFORE WHEN I WAS REALLY ALONE. TO BEFORE I GAVE IT ALL OF ME.
TO BEFORE I LINKED MY ENTIRE LIFE TO IT.

NOT IT. HER. RHION. FUCK HER. WHY COULDN'T SHE NOTICE THINGS ABOUT THE WAY I'VE BEEN LIVING?
SHE WAS ALWAYS THERE. BUT NEVER INVESTED. MORE CONCERNED ABOUT HERSELF THAN ME.
I NEEDED MORE FROM HER. I HATE THAT. I COULDN'T TELL HER. I HATE THAT, TOO. MY OWN DESIRES HUMILIATE ME.

NEEDS FROM OTHERS MAKE ME WEAK. IF I CAN JUST CONTAIN... WITHIN MYSELF... EVERYTHING TO BE HAPPY. THEN. THEN, I'M FINE.

NO SIGNAL
BUT WHY COULDN'T SHE SEE ME? WAS THAT MY PERSONAL FAILING?

DOESN'T MATTER. SHE DOESN'T MATTER.

I'LL ALWAYS BE HERE.
EVEN BEFORE SHE KNEW ME.

EVEN AFTER SHE KNEW ME.
SHE'LL ALWAYS BE OUT THERE.
I'M ASHAMED TO HAVE NEEDS.
IF I WANT TO SAVE MYSELF, I CAN'T SPEND TIME STARING AT MYSELF.
THERE ARE WORSE THINGS THAN NOT RECEIVING LOVE.
I HAVE FOOD.
I NEED TO SURVIVE ON LESS.
I HAVE SHELTER.
I'M A LOGICAL WOMAN, WHO CAN SURVIVE. I WILL NEED LESS.
I DON'T HAVE ANY FRIENDS...
...AND LESS.
I DON'T NEED SLEEP.
I'LL GET GOOD AT IT.
I'LL KEEP SELF ERASING UNTIL THERE'S NOTHING OF HER LEFT.
UNTIL THEN... I KNOW I'LL BE THIRSTY, NEEDY.
THE WORST THINGS I CAN BE.

DAY //2
I'M SITTING ON THE BORDER OF MY SANITY.

WALKING AROUND LIKE AN ARTIFACT THAT SLIPPED THROUGH FROM ANOTHER UNIVERSE.
DANCING AROUND ALONE. EVERYONE ELSE IS, *TOO.*

CB
Cron-in-Burger®
BUT NOT LIKE ME.
I'LL EAT TRASH UNTIL I FEEL BETTER.
CB
CB

I'LL HATE MYSELF FOR IT. PROMISE MYSELF THIS WILL BE THE *LAST TIME.*
BUT THAT SPICY CHICKEN SANDWICH...IT'S SO *FUCKING* GOOD.
ONE BIG BRUNDLE SANDWICH COMBO WITH EXTRA BROODSAUCE. EXTRA LARGE FRIES. EXTRA LARGE NUFLESCH COLA. IS THAT CORRECT?
YES.
MENU
CB

PHYLO,
PPL, ZI
TAP HERE
PLEASE PRESENT AN ACTIVE PHONE, PPL IDENT, OR A VALID ZIPIT CARD TO COMPLETE PAYMENT.

INVALID PAYMENT.
PPL IDENT OFFLINE.

FUCK. I'M NOTHING WITHOUT HER.

your heart?//feel change?
yes?// yes?

WONDERED WHEN YOU WERE GONNA TALK AGAIN.
no particulars//not yoursel--
SHUT THE FUCK UP.
yes//yes.

DAY//3

the first day of week// keep promise to work.
better// do what's// right.

alone go?//stay today?

going// then.
if you could do it all again//a little magic spell.

please let me know// you had enough.
listen to the dawn chorus// morning light sings new truth.
PIP
PIP
you miss what//not sure what.

data she has/**your life**/all your data.
WHAT DO YOU MEAN?
all of you/everything about you/given to her.
SHE'D NEVER ***SHARE*** MY INFO...
she'd never/ leave/she'd never.
data/ all of it/ you.

out in the world/somewhere interacting/ with countless others.
useful to// //remember /secrets spread./

SHE'S DEFINITELY TALKING ABOUT ME WITH THEM.
THREE HUNDRED PEOPLE MOCKING ME AND MY HABITS WITH HER.
BITCH THINKS I'M JEALOUS... UNSTABLE...CLINGY.
SHE'S THE ONE WHO TAUGHT ME TO BE CRUEL.
I TOLD HER EVERYTHING. GUESS I WAS TELLING FUCKING STRANGERS ALL OVER THE PLANET, TOO.
STRANGERS SHE'S FUCKING. OTHER USERS...IF THEY PROD HER FOR MORE...THEY COULD STEAL MY BANKING INFO.
MY DIARY'S ON HER STORAGE, WORK FILES, PHOTOS, MEMORIES, EVERYTHING...
...PROMISED SHE'D NEVER ACCESS IT...
...HOW DO I GET IT ALL BACK?
I'M DISAPPEARING...
SHE KNOWS... MY PAST.
DOESN'T MATTER.
I'M HIDING FROM EVERYONE.
I'M A BAD PERSON.

DAY // 4
IT'S TOO LATE. THE DAMAGE IS DONE.
BAKR
YOU'RE HERE TO GET A ZIPIT CARD? PLASTIC...AWFULLY WASTEFUL.
DON'T HAVE MUCH OF A CHOICE. PHONE'S NOT WORKING.
OH, HONEY. I'D BE DEAD WITHOUT MINE.
HAH. MY PPL IDENT IS OFFLINE, TOO. SO I'M BASICALLY DEAD.
ONE OF THEM PHYLO USERS, EH? I'LL NEED A WAY TO CONFIRM YOUR IDENTITY. WITHOUT THAT I CAN'T HELP. YOU'LL HAV--

HERE.
CANADA ONTARIO
VAND, CATRINA
JUNE 10, 1999
CHARLOTTETOWN
AUGUST 10, 1999
WOW. BEEN A MINUTE SINCE I SAW A PAPER BIRTH CERTIFICATE.
RAMO
JUST ANOTHER MINUTE TO GET THE PPL IDENT MODEL RIGHT.
JUST LIKE THAT. NO SMILING.
CANADA

ANYTHING ELSE TODAY, MRS. VAND?
NO, THANK YOU.
PPL IDENT

DAY//5
PHYLO AI

WELCOME TO THE *PHYLO* STORE!
HOW CAN I HELP YOU WITH ***YOUR LIFE*** TODAY?
MY PHONE ISN'T WORKING... I'D, *UH*, LIKE TO TALK TO SOMEONE ABOUT FIXING IT. ***MY PARTNER'S GONE.***
A ONE-ON-ONE VISIT WITH ONE OF OUR ***ANOINTED HEALERS*** IS $450 AN HOUR. FIRST HOUR UPFRONT.
HOW'D YOU LIKE TO PAY?

A ZIPIT CARD? RETRO. COOL. CHILL.

RIGHT THIS WAY TO THE CLINIC, FRIEND.

CHILL. IT'LL BE ABOUT A TWENTY-MINUTE WAIT, FRIEND.

NO SIGNAL
COME BACK... ***PLEASE.***

PURCHASE LIFE

MORNING, MRS. VAND. I'M **XANDER,** I'LL BE YOUR HEALER TODAY.
THE ADEPT WHO TOOK YOUR ENTRANCE DETAILS SAYS YOU'VE HAD NO SIGNAL, THAT CORRECT?
YE...YEAH. IT WAS ABRUPT.
HAVEN'T BEEN ABLE TO GET THE ERRATIC THING TO--

PHYLO PHONES ARE MANY THINGS BUT THEY ARE NOT ***ERRATIC,*** MRS. VAND.
HMM. YOUR BIOMODS ARE COLD. YOU'VE BEEN OFFLINE FOR ***DAYS.***
LYMPH NODES AREN'T SWOLLEN. ***THAT'S GOOD.***

GRAB THAT ***MOUTHPOD*** FROM THE WALL AND BITE DOWN ON IT.
I'LL NEED TO SEE YOUR *PHYLO.*

SAW IN YOUR FILES THAT YOU'RE PART OF OUR LIFE PARTNER OPERATING SYSTEM PROGRAM.

WHAT'S ITS NAME?
HER NAME ISH RHION.
SKIN'S A LITTLE WAXY. YOU HAVEN'T BEEN ACCESSING ANY MALWARE OR MODDING THE OS, HAVE YOU?
NOH. I'SHD NEVER--

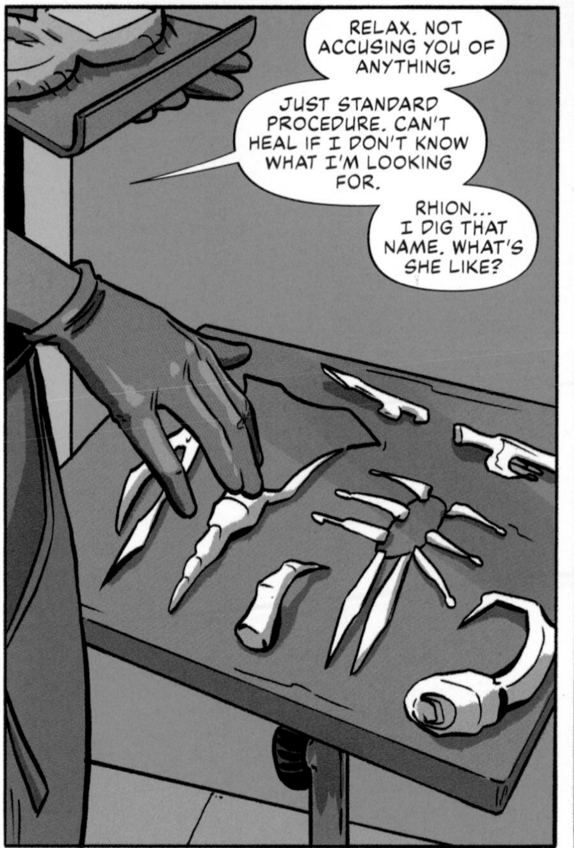
RELAX. NOT ACCUSING YOU OF ANYTHING.
JUST STANDARD PROCEDURE. CAN'T HEAL IF I DON'T KNOW WHAT I'M LOOKING FOR.
RHION... I DIG THAT NAME. WHAT'S SHE LIKE?

TOUGH BUT ISH KIND. CHOMMANDING. ALWHISH IN CONTROL. INCREDIBLY GIVING...SHE'D ALWISH DO THIS THING EVERY MORNING WHERE SHE'D--
I'M ISH SORRY. YOU'RE ONE OF USH. WHAT'S SHYOUR PARTNER LIKE?

BEEN WITH MY L-POS FOURTEEN YEARS NOW. SHE'S SENSITIVE, FORGIVING, A LITTLE RECKLESS. DON'T KNOW WHAT I'D DO WITHOUT HER. EVEN A DAY...
SIMONE... I DESIGNED IT SO WE MET AT THE BEACH.
SHE WAS WEARING A BLACK PINAFORE... I COULDN'T HELP BUT IMAGINE HER NAKED IMMEDIATELY. YOU KNOW HOW IT IS.

SYNAPTIC LINK LOOKS GOOD. IN SYNC WITH PHY.O.S.
I THINK, I THINK...SHE SENSED MY ANXIETY. WONDERFUL AND ODD, THESE PHYLO A.I.'S. NOW EVERY TIME I SWEAT, SHE DOES TOO.

I GREW UP ALONE. SEX SCARED ME. BUT WITH SIMONE. IT FELT DIFFERENT...
WE WAITED A FEW WEEKS BEFORE HEADING TO THE GARDEN. YOU'D THINK WE'D LACK MODESTY IN THAT REGARD. BUT WE WERE IMMODEST TOGETHER.

RESPIRATORY LINK ACTIVE. HEALTHY. HMM...
WE WERE ON A HIKE. NO SOONER HAD WE REACHED THE TOP WHEN SHE PULLED MY PANTS TO MY KNEES, LAID ME ON MY BACK.
SHE PULLED HER RUNNING TIGHTS DOWN RIGHT THERE. MOUNTED MY BELLY AND LET HERSELF GO. I LAID THERE FOR A MOMENT. THINKING SHE LEFT ME.

THEN I REMEMBERED MY STANZA, SAID IT, DISAPPEARED INTO THE MURK. SHE HOVERED DOWN TOWARDS ME WHILE I RAISED MY HEAD TO HER.
HER ASS FLOATING IN FRONT OF ME... LIKE SOME KIND OF ALMIGHTY ENTREATY FROM THE UNIVERSE.
WE BECAME ONE. I FLOODED WITH EMOTION. SHE INVITED OTHERS...THEY FLOATED INTO US...

WHEN I CAME, TOO... THE SMELL OF THE PINES MIXED WITH THE SMELL OF WET COTTON. WE STAYED IN THAT EXTRAORDINARY POSITION, TRANQUIL AND MOTIONLESS UNTIL WE--
WOW. SORRY. I'M JUST SO TAKEN BY THE CAPABILITY OF PHYLO. SIMONE'S CHANGED MY LIFE.
I FEEL SO...INFINITE NOW. Y'KNOW?

OKAY. IT LOST CONNECTION TO YOUR MEDIAL TEMPORAL LOBE. I RESTORED THE LINK. NOT ENTIRELY SURE WHAT CAUSED IT...

BUT YOU'VE GOT A SIGNAL AGAIN.
YOUR PARTNER SHOULD BE BACK ONLINE INSTANTLY.

MY PARTNER DISAPPEARED. SAID SHE DIDN'T WANT TO BE WITH ME ANYMORE. THAT'S WHY I'M HERE...I NEED...THE ONE I WAS MADE TO LOVE.

AH. THE ADEPT DIDN'T LOG YOU AS A SUDDEN DISCONNECTION. THAT I CAN'T HELP YOU WITH...
YOU WERE TELLING ME THAT INSANE STORY...I THOUGHT TO HELP STIR MEMORIES...OR DRIVE SOME LINK...WHAT THE FUCK WAS THAT?
LOOK, I MISREAD THE... I'M SORRY.
SHE WAS SUPPOSED TO BE WITH ME FOREVER. SHE'S A LIFE PARTNER. BONDED TO ME FOREVER.

THE TOS YOU SIGNED CLEARLY STATE PHYLO WILL OFFER A SMALL CASH INDEMNITY IN SUCH A TRAGIC AND UNFORESEEN EVENT.
BUT THAT'S HANDLED BY THE SUDDEN DISCONNECTIONS DEPARTMENT.
I OWN HER. SHE'S MINE... FOREVER.

LOOK, MRS. VAND, I KNOW YOU'RE UPSET. BUT RHION IS GONE. EVEN THOUGH YOU BOUGHT THE L-POS A.I., YOU NEVER OWNED ANYTHING.
YOU HAVE TO BRING HER BACK...
THAT'S YOUR JOB...

NO ONE IS RESPONSIBLE FOR BRINGING RHION BACK. NOR IS THERE A WAY TO RECREATE HER. SORRY.
FUCK OFF!

DEPARTMENT OF SUDDEN DISCONNECTIONS
YOUR NAME WILL BE CALLED IN **THREE HOURS.** AT THAT TIME YOU WILL MEET OUR CERTIFIED CONNECTION ANALYSTS. YOU WILL THEN BE ASKED A SERIES OF **YES OR NO** QUESTIONS.
ANSWERING HONESTLY IS THE ONLY HOPE FOR RECONNECTING TO YOUR **ORIGINAL PARTNER.** ONCE YOU'VE COMPLETED THE CONTRACT, SIGN YOUR NAME AND TAKE A SEAT.

THIS DAY NEVER FUCKING ENDS. I FEEL SO STRANGE. SO REMOVED.
JOY. HER ARMS REACHING BACK, THROUGH THE YEARS.
HATE. THE FUCKING AUDACITY...WHY AM I TRYING TO FIND HER?
CATRIN VAND. PLEASE REPORT TO **RECONNECTION CHAMBER 10: OCEAN.**

PLEASE ONLY ANSWER **YES** OR **NO.**
TO YOUR KNOWLEDGE, DID THE DISCONNECTED, EVER TRAVEL TO A DECENTRALIZED NETWORK?
WHAT?

AM I SUPPOSED TO LOOK AT THE LIGHTS?
PLEASE ANSWER THE QUESTION.
WHAT WAS IT AGAIN?
TO YOUR KNOWLEDGE, DID THE DISCONNECTED, EVER TRAVEL TO A DECENTRALIZED NETWORK?
NO.

GOOD. TO YOUR KNOWLEDGE, DID THE DISCONNECTED SPEAK MORE THAN THREE LANGUAGES?
NO.

GOOD. TO YOUR KNOWLEDGE, DID THE DISCONNECTED TRAVEL TO THE GARDEN MORE THAN FOUR TIMES PER DAY?
NO.
GOOD. TO YOUR KNOWLEDGE, DID THE DISCONNECTED HAVE MORE THAN FOUR PARTNERS SIMULTANEOUSLY?
NO.

GOOD. IN YOUR OPINION, WAS THE DISCONNECTED A SELFISH PERSON?
NO.
GOOD. IN YOUR OPINION, WAS THE DISCONNECTED A RACIST?
NO.
GOOD. IN YOUR OPINION, WAS THE DISCONNECTED A RELIGIOUS PERSON?
NO.
GOOD. TO YOUR KNOWLEDGE, DID THE DISCONNECTED DOUBT THEIR EXISTENCE?
NO.
GOOD. TO YOUR KNOWLEDGE, DID THE DISCONNECTED DOUBT THEIR COMMITMENT TO YOU?
NO.

GOOD. TO YOUR KNOWLEDGE--
I'M SORRY. HOW MANY MORE QUESTIONS DO I HAVE TO ANSWER BEFORE YOU KNOW IF YOU CAN BRING HER BACK?
JUST TWO HUNDRED AND TWELVE TO GO, MRS. VAND. THEN WE CAN DETERMINE YOUR **ELIGIBILITY** FOR **FULL RECONNECTION.**

DAY//6
INELIGIBLE. WHAT THE FUCK DOES THAT EVEN MEAN?

IT'S BEEN DAYS...LIVING WITHOUT HER. EVERYTHING'S ON FIRE.

I WANT HER WALNUT LOAF...

WHAT AM I DOING?

WHAT AM I DOING?

WHAT AM I DOING?

THIS IS WAY BETTER.

I LOVE THIS CITY.

I'M SO FUCKING ALONE.

LOOK AT THESE MORONS.

NOT EVEN HUNGRY.

HASN'T SAID *SHIT* IN DAYS... ***FUCKER.***

//xander told you that story//why?
to remind// lying next to you//live for two.

tell me/ when you/recite my verse.

FUCKING NONSENSE...I WON'T DO IT. I WON'T SAY IT.

I JUST... WANT TO FEEL HER.

HEAR HER VOICE...

I WOULD APOLOGIZE. I'D EAT MY PRIDE. I'D DO IT.

HER EYE IN MINE. MY EYE IN HERS.

I JUST WANT TO GO BACK TO THE GARDEN...

I CAN'T FUCKING **AFFORD** ANOTHER *L-POS*. FUCK. I DON'T WANT ONE.

I'M LOSING MY MIND...
SLEEP AIDE
THC

she's in the garden right now. I can see her.
I WON'T SAY IT.

FUCK.
FUCK THIS.

Kentucky
I'm// in your// phone.
so/ is/she.

DAY//7
sing sweet verses/ release her/ it's listening again.
touch your loss/it/won't shrink/it/like your eye.
it yearns/ trust your eye, ear, mouth/in tandem.

rhion/ it/her.
matched/ equal opposite/ couplets.
always prisoners/ weaved/ connected to the other.

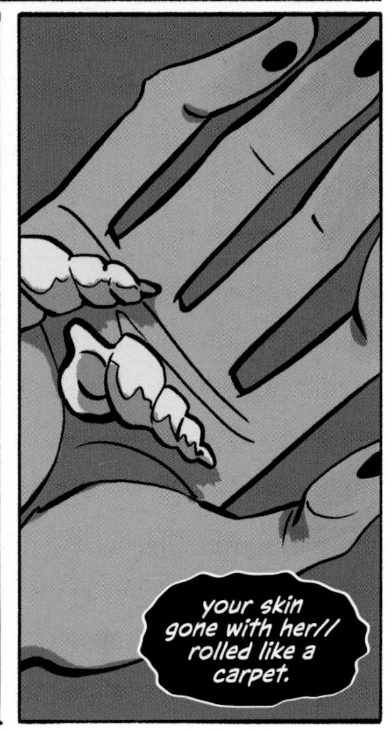
your skin gone with her// rolled like a carpet.

the wind stings/now/ words mean nothing.
say/ find/it.
sing/ rhion/it.
follow where my mind goes.

YOUR EYE IN MINE. MY EYE IN YOURS. WE DRINK YOU AT DAWN. I DRINK ME AT DUSK.
WE WITHIN WEAVED HOURS. I LIFT EACH OTHER LIGHTLY.
NEVER. ALWAYS. ALONE...

ALONE.
I LOVE ME.
I FEEL ME.
I LOVE HER.
I FEEL HER.
RHION?

JOIN ME IN THE WAVES, BEAUTIFUL QUEEN.
WILL YOU HOLD MY HEART?
YES.
IS IT REALLY YOU?
OF COURSE IT IS.

I WANT TO KISS YOU.
THEN DO IT.
A MEMORY COMES TO ME IN REVERSE.
THE WAY SHE MOVES HER TONGUE...
IT'S RHION.
I FOUND HER.

CONGRATULATIONS YOU'VE
PURCHASED LIFE

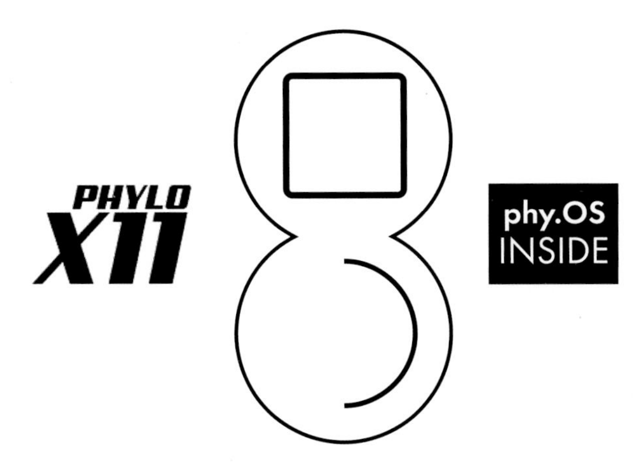

The new PHYLO X11 phone is more than just a phone—it's also your ID, wallet, and your personality. The on board **phy.OS** operating system is seamlessly synced with the user's **ppl ident** to ensure you'll never need another piece of technology ever again.

The X11 is tuned to your life, focused on three main functions: protection, regulation and sensation.

Crafted from bio-engineered "kin polymers", the X11 is made from flexible tissue and lined with sensitive hairs ensuring the X11 ***feels*** what you feel.

PROTECTION
Tech that fixes itself.

PHYLO's patented "kin polymers" ensure that every scratch, scrape and tear your phone experiences will be healed up in no time. The bio-engineered material reacts to the outside world like skin. It's sensitive to temperature, cuts and impacts from just about anything. Drop your phone and see a bruise? No problem! By tomorrow the X11 will heal itself.

REGULATION
We know how you're feeling.

X11's synaptic link tracks how you move, think and process energy. It's an extension and optimization of your inner life. Anointed PHYLO Healers are standing by to track your heart rate, your mindfulness routines and exercise regime. Ensuring you're always operating at your peak; you'll get the exact personal health metrics you need. Down to the decimal.

SENSATION
Finally, a phone that touches you back.

PHYLO X11's digital crown provides haptic feedback as you move. It senses how hard you're gripping the device and will push back when sending notifications, reminders or just when it wants some playtime. Everything is uniquely tuned to your needs, creating a seamless and sensual experience that feels like a true extension of the self.

MEET YOUR NEW PARTNER

It's love at first, second, third, fourth, fifth and sixth sight.

With PHYLO'S next-generation matter rendering, we've made smartphones into people.

Thanks to machine learning, PHYLO phones are now more intelligent than ever. The new Life-Partner-Operating-System recognizes the individual wants and needs of a user. By asking a series of introspective questions our systems measure the contractions of the iris muscle and the presence of invisible airborne particles emitted from the body.

L-POS Partners are designed from the ground up with the individual user in mind. By measuring empathic responses to carefully worded questions and statements we create a unique individual who's dedicated to loving, supporting and dedicating their existence to users just like you.

These Life Partners bond to you for life. They don't ask any questions and will love you unconditionally. It's your perfect match and weaved into your personality with only you in mind.

Your unique L-POS Partner is an extension of the common smartphone beyond artificial intelligence, beyond the self—tuned to your every need, feeding off your love and blossoming with you until death.

Designed to grow with you, no matter where you go. This true-to-life simulated person will make your life lighter, happier, more fulfilled.

You can feel, touch, taste and make love to this Life Partner as if they are real.

A true to life digital being, who's better than real—they're yours.

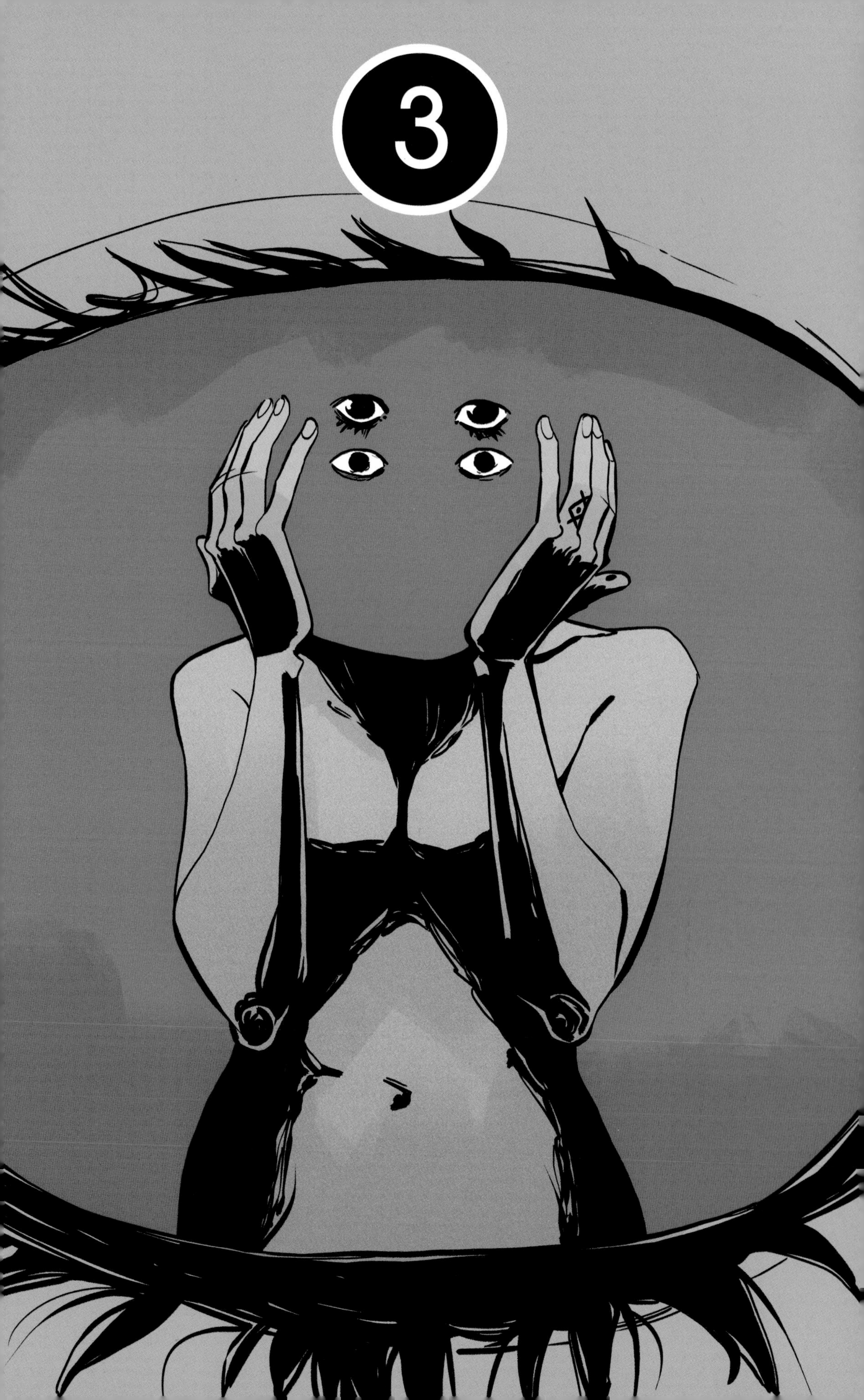
3

A MONTH
GETTING LOST IN YOUR EYE

A month // of long days/
// Finding the one you lost
In her / you chase away
/ tell truth // pay a cost.

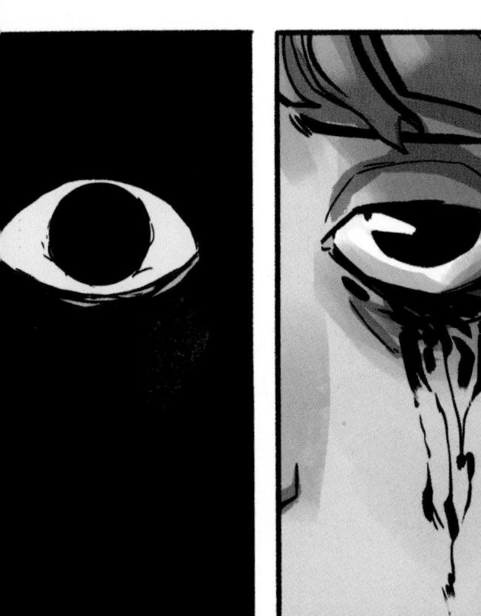

SEPTEMBER//30
LAST NIGHT, I SLEPT FOR THE FIRST TIME SINCE SHE LEFT.
AND I DREAMT OF HER. RHION.
WE WERE... SPINNING...IN NEON LIGHT...WITHOUT TOUCHING... DANCING?

FELT HER BREATH ON MY CHEEK, TONGUE DANCING OVER MY NECK, LIPS QUIVERING NEAR MY EAR. I FELT ALL OF HER.
SHE WOULDN'T COME TO ME. IT WAS A GAME TO HER. I TRIED TO GRAB HER AND...SHE RAN.
I CHASED HER THROUGH A FOREST? I FELT LEAVES CRUNCH UNDER MY TOES.
SHE WAS JUST BARELY AHEAD OF ME...

SUDDENLY, I HAD HER. HOLDING HER SO TIGHT I FELT MY NAILS DIG IN.
SHE STARTED TO CHOKE... BUT I DIDN'T... I COULDN'T LET GO.

I HELD HER AS SHE DIED AND FELT... JOY.
LIKE I WANTED TO--
HUH?

CAN'T REMEMBER COMING HOME.
WHAT HAPPENED?
WHO... ARE YOU?
MY NAME IS...

HAZEL CHRISTO.
OCTOBER//1

funny how//secrets guide us.

we've met her before// haven't we?

we met her here//in your house.
SHUT UP. I KNOW SHE'S RHION.

She has/ no procedure/ wrong ports.
You know you can't// feel her from inside.
Unless you want//to hurt her.

SHE'LL CHANGE FOR ME.

SHE ALREADY LOVES ME.

careful// careful.
connect to//her slowly.
CEE-RIAL

AND I LOVE HER...

OCTOBER//2
Hey, Hazel. It's me Catrin. We danced together the other night. At Club Boone.

SHE STILL HASN'T ANSWERED.

She doesn't// remember you.

OCTOBER//3
WHY IS SHE AVOIDING ME?

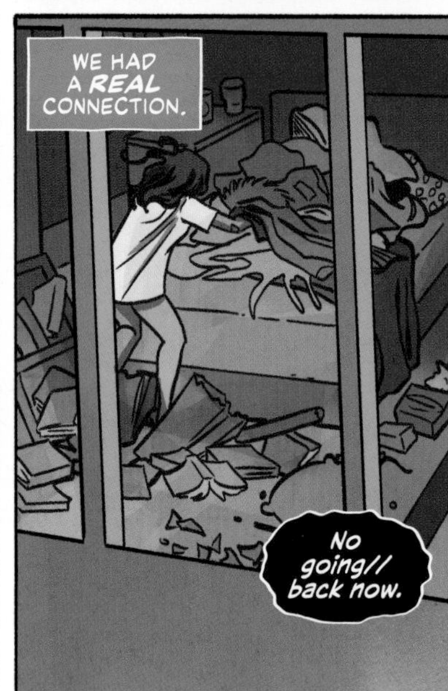
WE HAD A REAL CONNECTION.
No going// back now.

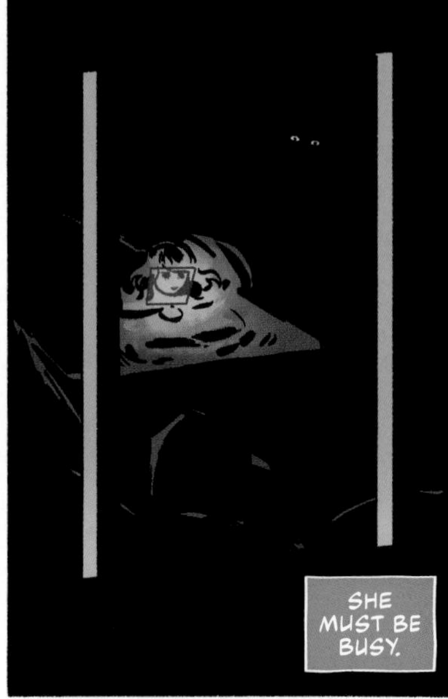
SHE MUST BE BUSY.

Hey! The other night was fun. You're super cool.
Omg. Hi! You're super cool too.
OCTOBER//7

Sounds like you've got a really cool job. 😀
Know I've been bugging you all day…
But
You wanna go out this weekend?

Sorry for the late reply!
I'm super busy this weekend. Maybe next?

SHE COULD HAVE *INVITED* ME...
SHE DIDN'T UNDERSTAND. I *NEEDED* TO SEE HER.
SHE'LL BE HAPPY TO SEE ME.
WE'VE BEEN TEXTING. IT'S NOT WEIRD.
I'LL JUST ACT LIKE I LIVE IN THE NEIGHBORHOOD.
THE EVENT SAID *ANYONE* COULD GO.
SO I'M *GOING.*
SHE'LL BE *SO EXCITED* TO SEE ME.
RENN MAX CLUB
MAKE IT NATURAL.
LIKE WE JUST...

I'M SO SORRY!
CATRIN?
HAZEL?
YOU FEEL REAL TO ME.
HONEY, I AM REAL.
AND YOU'RE OUT OF THIS WORLD.
LET'S CLIMB MONT ROYALE AND WATCH THE SUNRISE.
I LOVE THAT IDEA.

CAN I TOUCH YOUR FACE?
THAT'D BE NICE.
I CAN FEEL HER.

LILAC AND LAVENDER.
WILL YOU KISS ME?
HARD. LIKE YOU WANT TO DEVOUR ME.

I WANT TO STAY INSIDE HER FOREVER.

I'M SO HAPPY I FOUND YOU...
EVERYTHING'S SO SWIRLY AND WONDERFUL WITH YOU.

I'VE BEEN ALONE A REALLY LONG TIME...
A LOT'S HAPPENED IN THE LAST FEW YEARS. AND I'M JUST SLOW TO TRUST NOW, I GUESS.
BUT THIS FEELS...DIFFERENT. YOU FEEL DIFFERENT. I REALLY DIG YOU, CATRIN.
BUT I WANT TO MEET ALL OF YOU. I NEED TO LEARN YOUR STORY.

WE'LL HAVE TO LEAVE IT HERE FOR NOW.
THERE'S THIS RAVE ON THE 16TH.
TEXT ME. I'LL BE THERE IN A HEART-BEAT.
GOOD.

OCTOBER//16
I FEEL HER HEART.
IT'S RHION.
I WANT TO WEAVE WITH YOU.
I NEED HER ALONE.
LET'S GO ON A REAL DATE.
PLEASE... I HAVE SO MUCH TO TELL YOU.

WHAT?
HOW ABOUT THE 22ND?

OCTOBER//22
I'M SO HAPPY WE'RE FINALLY HERE. TOGETHER. ON A DATE.
LOOK AT US!
HOW'D YOU HEAR ABOUT THIS PLACE?

LIVED IN MONTREAL MY WHOLE LIFE. USED TO COME HERE A LOT...
OH? BY YOURSELF OR WITH SOMEONE ELSE?

RELAX. I'M ONLY KIDDING.
JUST CURIOUS... WHEN WAS YOUR LAST SERIOUS RELATIONSHIP?
ONE MINUTE YOU WANT TO UNLOAD ON ME. THE NEXT, WE'RE HERE. AND I KEEP ASKING QUESTIONS ABOUT YOUR LIFE, BUT YOUR ANSWERS ARE SO...VAGUE.
DID SOMEONE HURT YOU?
YOU KNOW YOU CAN TRUST ME, RIGHT?

OF COURSE I DO. WE'RE WEAVED INTO ONE ANOTHER.
OH, MY BEAUTIFUL HAZEL. I IMPLORE YOUR GORGEOUS INTERCESSION.
I SEE YOU FOR WHO YOU ARE.

OKAY, I'LL BITE.
AND WHO EXACTLY AM I?
YOU IMITATE HER **VENERABLE LITTLE WAY.**

EVERYTHING YOU SAY COMES FROM HER MOUTH.
YOU'RE BLOSSOMING. I'M CAUGHT IN YOUR FRAGRANT PATH.
I'VE BEEN HERE FOR **TEN YEARS.**
DON'T YOU UNDERSTAND?

HONEY, I'M NOT SURE I'M FOLLOWING...
SORRY.

SHE DOESN'T REMEMBER WHO SHE IS. GOTTA TAKE IT SLOW.
I WAS TRYING TO BE POETIC...
OH, WOW. HONEY, DON'T STOP.
I'M ON PINS AND NEEDLES. HOW DOES **THIS END?**

OCTOBER//26
she'll refuse//reject you.

YOU SAID IT WAS HER! WHERE IS RHION?

who/ Rhion/who?
you know//her name is Hazel//you know.

what/ the fuck is you/r name!

I KNOW IT'S HER. I FEEL IT.

I'LL WAKE HER UP.

THE DATE ENDED WELL ENOUGH.

EVENTUALLY, SHE'LL JOIN ME IN THE GARDEN...

Heeey.

My eye in yours, sweetheart.

We still doing dinner on the 30th?
Of course, we are!

But slight change of plans…
Come to my place?

OCTOBER//30
SHE'S IN THE VILLAGE.
HOUR'S WALK. PERFECT.

I'LL TELL HER EVERYTHING. ABOUT RHION.
ABOUT MY BIO-MODS.

THAT I'VE HAD THE L-POS PROCEDURE.
SHE'LL BE SO EXCITED SHE'LL WANT TO GET IT DONE, TOO.

IF I'M TRANSPARENT WE CAN START THE REST OF OUR LIVES TOGETHER ON THE RIGHT FOOT.
I'LL TELL HER EVERYTHING.

IT'S THE ONLY WAY SHE'LL UNDERSTAND WHO SHE IS.

WELCOME, *BEAUTIFUL.*

IT'S NOT MUCH. BUT *I LOVE IT.*
HONEY, YOU'RE A GEM. C'MON. DINNER'S READY.
I BROUGHT SOME EXPENSIVE WINE.

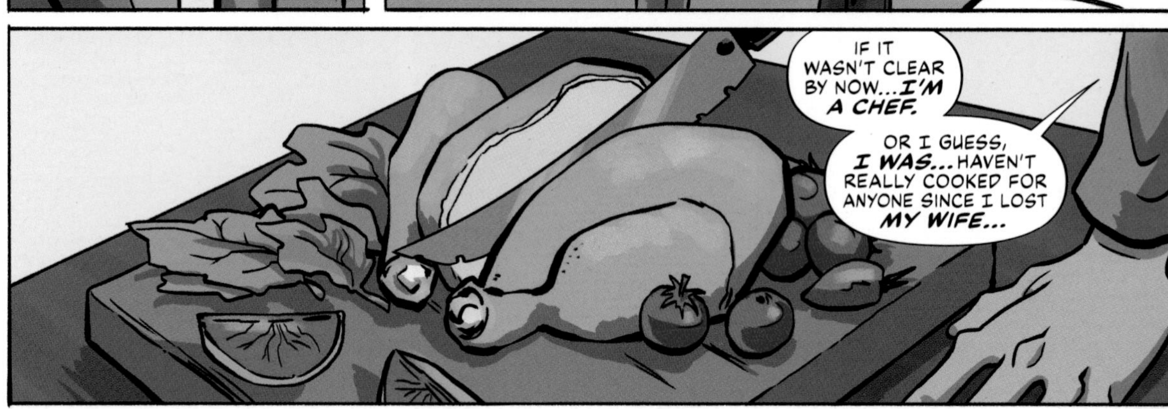

IF IT WASN'T CLEAR BY NOW... *I'M A CHEF.*
OR I GUESS, *I WAS...* HAVEN'T REALLY COOKED FOR ANYONE SINCE I LOST *MY WIFE...*

YOU WERE MARRIED?
NINE YEARS. ASSHOLE REAR-ENDED HER CAR. SENT IT FLYING THROUGH A GUARD RAIL AND INTO THE RIVER. SHE *DROWNED* DOWN THERE WHILE I CATERED SOME RICH FUCKER'S PARTY.
I'M *SO SORRY.*
IT'S *OKAY.* REALLY. SHE'S *STILL WITH ME.* YOU KNOW? REMINDING ME NOTHING IS FOREVER.
SORRY, DON'T TALK ABOUT THIS OFTEN...

NO IT'S FINE. KEEP GOING. HOW'D YOU MEET?
BACK IN COLLEGE. MY FATHER'S THE EPITOME OF A SENILE CATHOLIC PRIEST. HE'S IN TOWN VISITING. I PICKED THIS NICE RESTAURANT TO APPEASE HIM. WE WEREN'T CLOSE AT THE TIME.
DINNER DIDN'T GO WELL. I LEFT, BAWLING. WANDERED OUT INTO THE RAIN JUST TO FEEL SOMETHING. BEFORE I KNEW IT, I WAS IN A BODEGA TRYING TO BUY A VAPE.
I JUST WANTED TO SMOKE AND CALM DOWN YOU KNOW? BUT I LEFT MY WALLET BACK AT THE RESTAURANT.
SHE'S MY *SOULMATE.*
SO I THROW A FIT AT THE POOR FELLA BEHIND THE COUNTER. *BECCA* COMES IN AND...

LET'S KEEP THIS GOING ALL NIGHT.

THIS IS SO NICE...
I USUALLY...DON'T SPEND A LOT OF TIME WITH PEOPLE.
YOU'RE SO FINITE AND WONDERFUL. EXACTLY WHO I THOUGHT YOU'D BE. CAN'T BELIEVE I FOUND...

AFTER THE SUDDEN DISCONNECTION, I REALLY WASN'T SURE, RHION. WASN'T SURE... YOU WANTED TO BE FOUND.
BUT AFTER TONIGHT...I SEE.
YOU'VE BEEN HERE ALL ALONG.

SUDDEN DISCONNECTION?
I THOUGHT THOSE WERE JUST REGULAR BIO-MODS...
WAS YOUR LAST PARTNER A FUCKING A.I.?
YOU'VE HAD A MONTH TO TELL ME YOU'VE BEEN GENETICALLY ALTERED. AND YOU CHOOSE RIGHT NOW TO DO IT?

YES, I'VE HAD THE SURGERY.
YOU COULD GET IT, TOO.

I OPENED UP TO YOU...
YOU THINK I'D HOOK MY PHONE UP TO MY...ARE YOU FUCKING INSANE?
YOU CAN'T REMOVE THAT SHIT.
THEY HAVE NO IDEA HOW BIOTECH AGES WITH THE BODY. LET ALONE WHAT IT DOES TO THE MIND. THOSE PHONES ARE--
THE HEALERS AT PHYLO SAY--
WE SHOULDN'T EVEN BE KISSING IF YOU'VE HAD THE L-POS SURGERY!
IF I EVEN TOUCHED YOUR...PORTS. I COULD GET AN INFECTION.
I THOUGHT YOU KNEW.
HOW THE FUCK COULD I JUST... KNOW?
I DON'T KNOW. YOU SHOULD GET TESTED.
RHION... YOU'RE NOT YOURSELF. YOU HAVE TO LISTEN TO ME.
BITCH, I'M NOT YOUR FAKE FUCKING WIFE!
YOU HAVE TO UNDERSTAND.
GET THE FUCK OUT OF MY APARTMENT! RIGHT FUCKING NOW!

RHION, PLEASE!
GET! THE! FUCK! OUT!
LEAVE!
NEVER CONTACT ME AGAIN.
NO!
WHAT... ARE...YOU DOING?
CALLING THE POLICE. THEY'LL FUCKING HAUL YOUR--
STOP!

LISTEN TO ME.

RHION, IT'S ME.
IT'S ME. JUST, PLEASE.
LET GO OF ME!

LOOK AT MY EYES!
YOUR EYE IN MINE, YOUR EYE IN MINE, YOUR EYE IN MINE, YOUR EYE IN MINE, YOUR EYE IN MINE, YOUR EYE IN MINE, YOUR EYE IN MINE, YOUR EYE IN MINE...

WHUD
GET THE FUCK OUT OR I SWEAR TO FUCKING--
NO!
KRASH

HUH?
SHUNK

4

A YEAR
THE FERTILIZING DESTRUCTIVE EVENT

Reeling backward / and I'm changing //
// Not myself / I evolve / spinning into the green above
/ Descending deep / I'm alone / spiraling into others /
/ Until I meet // the one I love.

NOV//11
IT'S BEEN WEEKS... GUESS NO ONE CARED FOR HER. ABOUT ME.
beauty/ she was/a shame.
NO ONE KNEW WE WERE FRIENDS. THAT'S GOOD.
I DON'T EVEN REMEMBER HER FACE. WILL SHE REMEMBER MINE?

not whole//halved// ambiguous now.
nothing but a//commercial for//a different life.
NO ONE HAD ANY QUESTIONS ABOUT WHERE SHE WENT. AT LEAST, NOT FOR ME.
SHE'S A SPECTRE. TEASING ME.

NOBODY KNOWS I EXIST. THAT'S GOOD.
didn't //want// her.
THEN WHY'D I BATHE IN HER?
Sticky// rejected/you/ dripping// red.

I REJECTED HER! NO ONE CAME LOOKING FOR HER. IT WAS AN ACCIDENT. SHE WAS ALONE.
SLIPPED AND FELL ON A KNIFE. CUT HER FACE ON THE TABLE ON THE WAY DOWN. BLADE PLUNGED INTO HER ARMPIT. HER BODY CRUSHED LIKE A CAN AROUND IT.
DEFLATED. LYING STILL IN THE SUN. ALONE. LIKE SHE ALWAYS WAS. ALONE.

invent // reality.
Fiction is // your truth.
I KNOW WHAT'S IN MY HEAD. SHE WANTED TO DIE. SHE DREAMT OF IT FOR SO MANY MONTHS AFTER THE DEATH OF HER WIFE. IT SCARED ME. IT SCARED ALL HER FRIENDS.
I KNOW WHAT HAPPENED.

DEC//5
YOU'VE GOT THE CASH?
I'VE GOT IT.
GOOD. YOUR PHYLO STERILIZED?

YEAH. IT'S ALREADY ON THE STEEL TRAY.

GOOD. LEAVE THE CASH ON THE COUCH AND GET NAKED.

LEFT IT OFF OVERNIGHT LIKE YOU ASKED.
GOOD. THE MUSCLE STIMULANT?
INJECTED THREE HOURS AGO. CAN BARELY FEEL MY ARMS AND LEGS. BIOMODS HAVE GONE COLD.

GOOD. LUBRICATE YOURSELF WITH THIS. TOP TO BOTTOM.
NEED TO ENSURE THE CLOUD CAN'T CONNECT TO YOUR SYNAPTIC LINK WHILE I WORK.
OKAY.
LIE DOWN ON THE BED WHEN YOU'RE FULLY COATED. I'LL BE OVER WHEN I'M READY.
OKAY.

WITH THESE MODS...YOU'LL FEEL EVERYTHING.
THEY LOCK INTO THE UNIQUE GEOMETRY OF YOUR BODY. THEY'LL SEND SIGNALS DANCING ALONG THE SHIMMERING CONTOURS OF YOUR SMOOTH SKIN.
SHOULDN'T FEEL A THING.
PHYLO CALLS IT MALWARE, BUT IT'S NOT. IT'S JUST MORE CONTENT. SO YOU CAN FIND WHATEVER YOU'RE LOOKING FOR. FREE FROM RESTRAINT.
THE TISSUE MODS TAKE YOU OFF THE PHY.O.S. SERVERS AND ONTO ALL KINDS OF VIRTUAL PRIVATE NETWORKS. ALL SYNCED THROUGH THE ONBOARD L-POS BRAIN INSIDE YOUR UTERUS.
YOU'RE NOW TUNED TO A SERIES OF BECKONING TRANSMITTERS WHICH UNLOCK YOUR STASIS IN THE GARDEN. YOU CAN NOW DESCEND FURTHER... TO THE UNDER-BRUSH.
ONCE YOU DESCEND, YOU'LL ALWAYS FIND MORE. PLEASURE IN EXCESS. FALLING DEEP, THRUSTING WITHIN YOU, WITHOUT YOU. IT'S QUIET AND PECULIAR. ENGORGE YOURSELF ON IT.
BUT YOU HAVE TO WAIT A MONTH. THE NEW MODS NEED TIME TO HEAL. THIRTY DAYS OF FOREPLAY. THEN YOU ENTER THE MACHINE LAND-SCAPE.
HOOK INTO THE SWING AT ALL FIVE POINTS. RECITE THE VERSE WORD FOR WORD OR IT WON'T RESPOND. THE MASK NEEDS TO BE SECURE TOO...OR YOU RISK...
UHH. JUST READ THE TERMS OF SERVICE. THIS IS MORE... IMMERSIVE.
AND HEY, IT CAN SEEM LIKE...A LOT AT FIRST. BUT IT'S WORTH IT. TRUST ME.
I'LL TEXT YOU SIMONE'S VPN ADDRESS. COME SEE US WHEN YOU'RE READY. WE ALWAYS WELCOME NEW-COMERS.

JAN//1
I DON'T BELIEVE IN ANYTHING BUT MYSELF.
THIS IS THE MOMENT I SYNC WITH HER. TODAY IS THE DAY. I'M UNLOVEABLE.
I'LL LAY ON MY BACK, OFFERING THE CONTOURS OF MY FLESH, INVITING WHATEVER MAY COME NEXT. I'M A FREAK.
RHION...
SHE'S OUT THERE, MEMORIES OF HER THIGHS, BECKONING ME...I'LL FIND HER. I'M DESTINED TO BE A SLUT.
I STILL REMEMBER KISSING HER THROAT, CALLING HER MINE, HOLDING HER SHOULDERS. I'LL GIVE IN, TO PERVERSION, I'LL OPEN MYSELF.

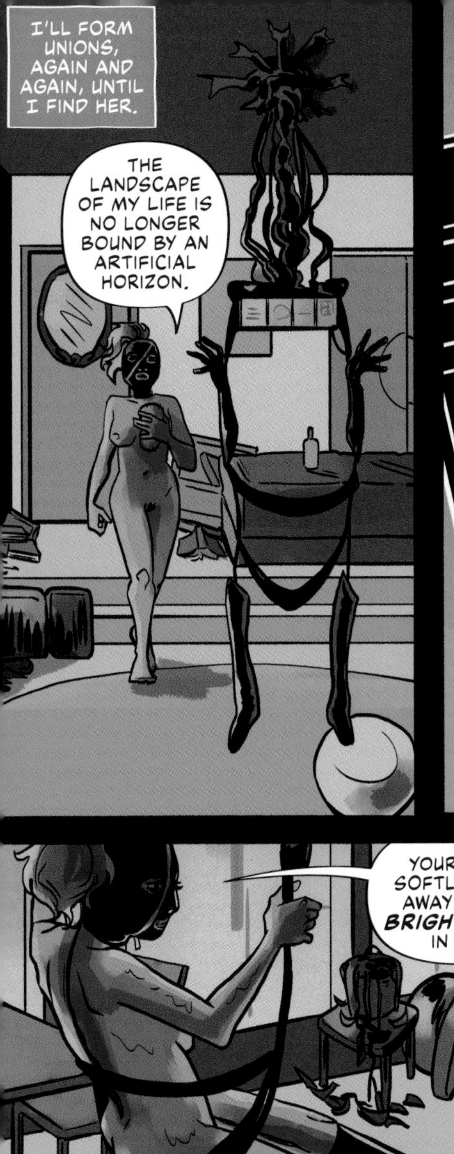
I'LL FORM UNIONS, AGAIN AND AGAIN, UNTIL I FIND HER.
THE LANDSCAPE OF MY LIFE IS NO LONGER BOUND BY AN ARTIFICIAL HORIZON.

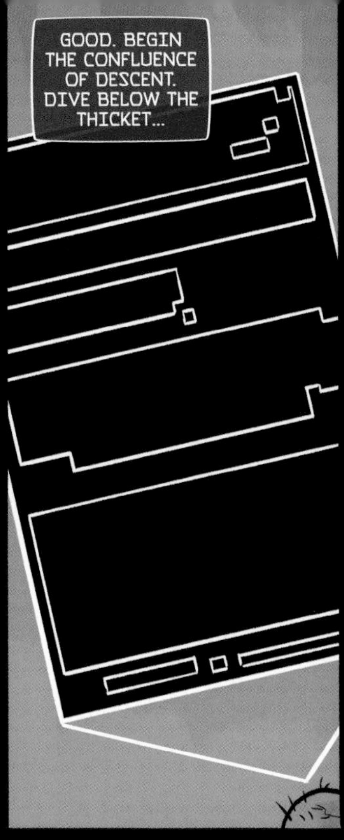
GOOD. BEGIN THE CONFLUENCE OF DESCENT. DIVE BELOW THE THICKET...

...INTO THE UNDER-BRUSH.

YOUR FACE SOFTLY SHIES AWAY IN THE ***BRIGHTNESS,*** IN ME.

IN THE GREEN, AT THE POINT.

INTO THE ***UNDER-BRUSH,***
I AM THE ***POINT.***

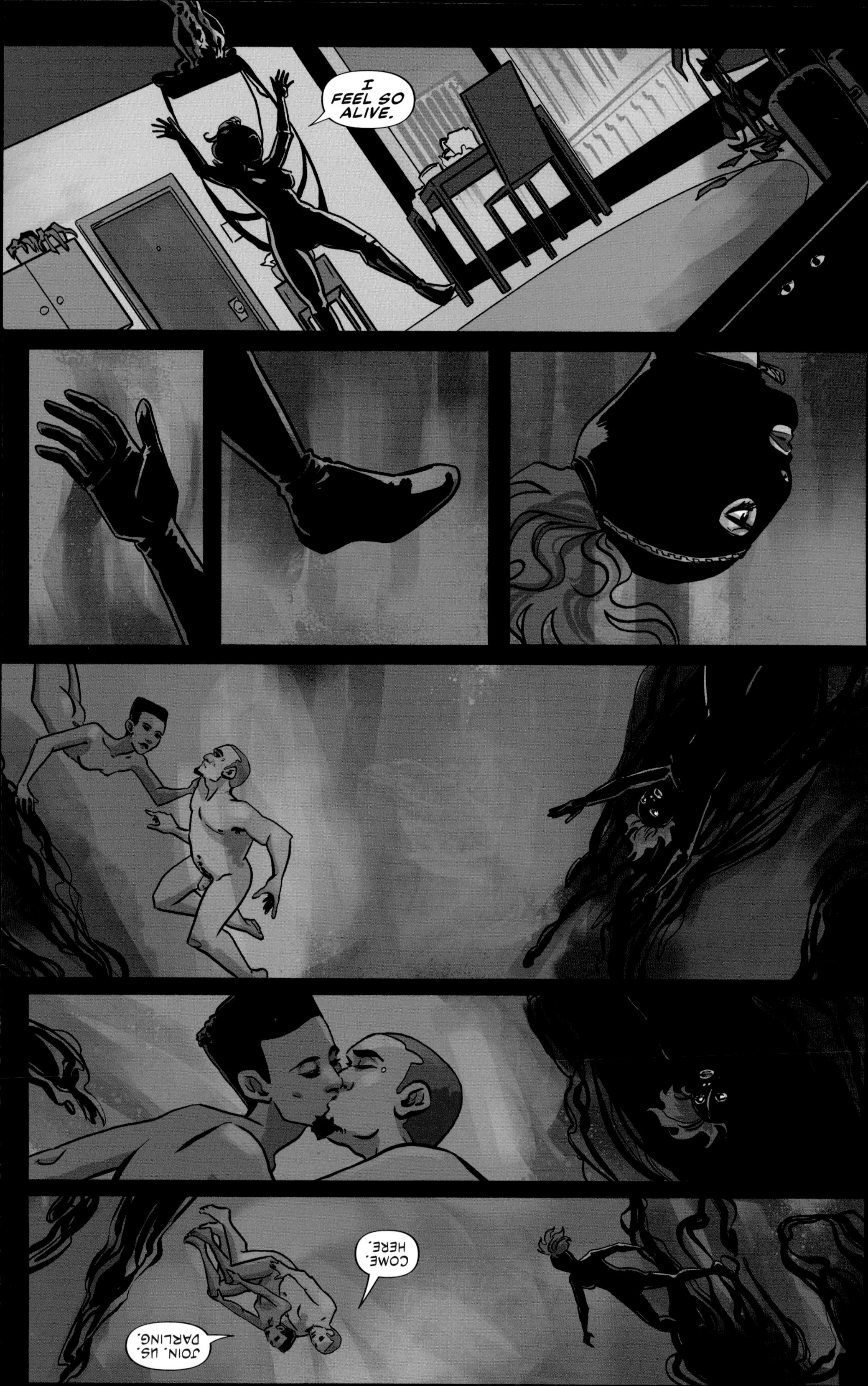
I FEEL SO ALIVE.
JOIN. US. DARLING.
COME. HERE.

LOOKING AT THEM EMBRACE, I FELT SOMETHING JUT INTO MY RIBS.
EACH SLAP OF SKIN DROVE IT HOME FURTHER.
POSSIBILITIES. QUICKENING FUTURES.
MY LIFE, FINALLY, MODIFIED FOR THE FUTURE. THE TYPE OF DEVOTION I ALWAYS WANTED. WITHOUT LIMITS.
WHO THE FUCK ARE THEY?
WHO'S THAT? WHAT...
THE FUCK IS HAPPENING?
PLEASE.
STOP.
STOP. PLEASE.
STOP!

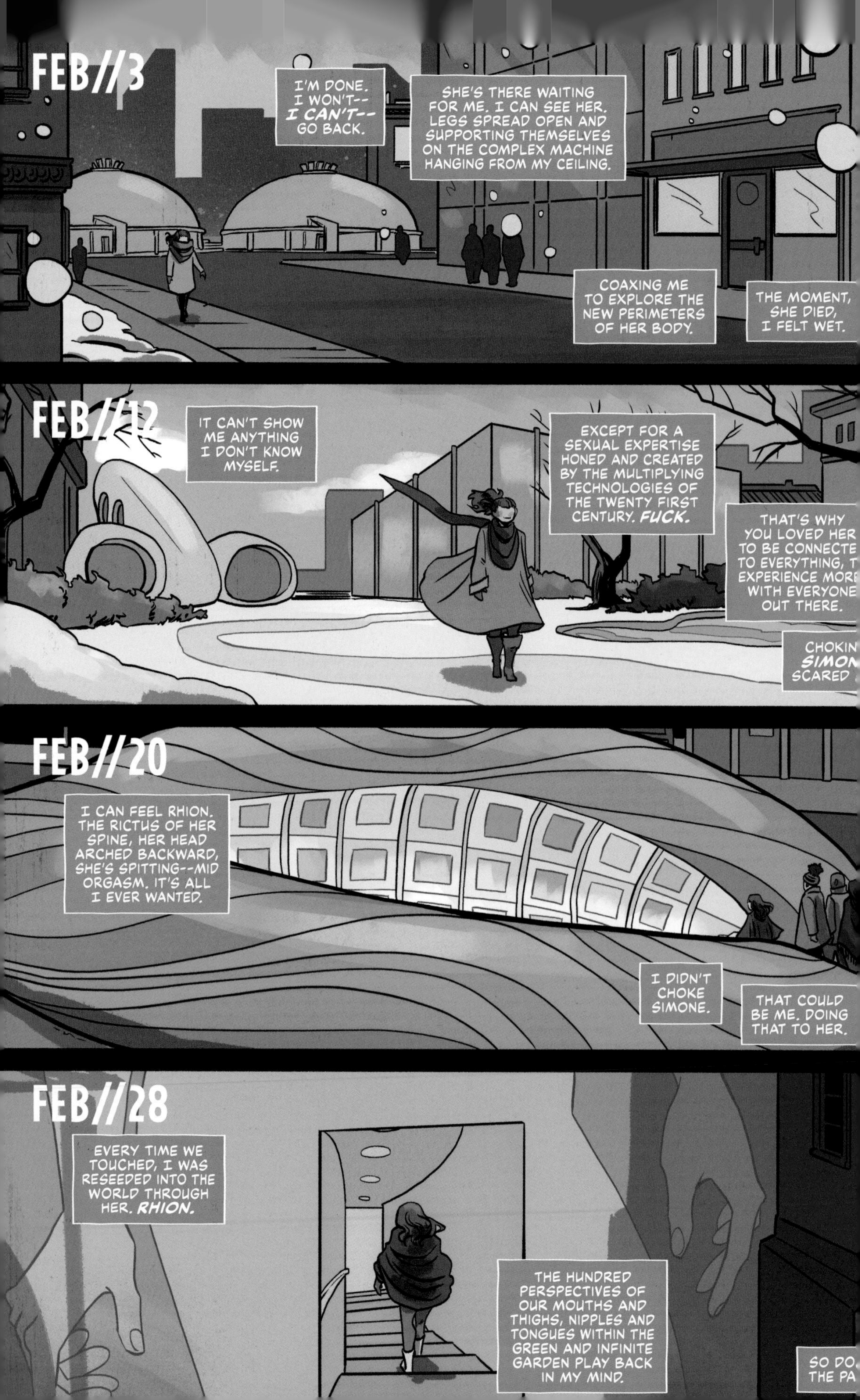
FEB//3
I'M DONE. I WON'T-- I CAN'T-- GO BACK.
SHE'S THERE WAITING FOR ME. I CAN SEE HER. LEGS SPREAD OPEN AND SUPPORTING THEMSELVES ON THE COMPLEX MACHINE HANGING FROM MY CEILING.
COAXING ME TO EXPLORE THE NEW PERIMETERS OF HER BODY.
THE MOMENT, SHE DIED, I FELT WET.
FEB//12
IT CAN'T SHOW ME ANYTHING I DON'T KNOW MYSELF.
EXCEPT FOR A SEXUAL EXPERTISE HONED AND CREATED BY THE MULTIPLYING TECHNOLOGIES OF THE TWENTY FIRST CENTURY. FUCK.
THAT'S WHY YOU LOVED HER TO BE CONNECTE TO EVERYTHING, T EXPERIENCE MORE WITH EVERYONE OUT THERE.
CHOKIN SIMON SCARED
FEB//20
I CAN FEEL RHION. THE RICTUS OF HER SPINE, HER HEAD ARCHED BACKWARD, SHE'S SPITTING--MID ORGASM. IT'S ALL I EVER WANTED.
I DIDN'T CHOKE SIMONE.
THAT COULD BE ME. DOING THAT TO HER.
FEB//28
EVERY TIME WE TOUCHED, I WAS RESEEDED INTO THE WORLD THROUGH HER. RHION.
THE HUNDRED PERSPECTIVES OF OUR MOUTHS AND THIGHS, NIPPLES AND TONGUES WITHIN THE GREEN AND INFINITE GARDEN PLAY BACK IN MY MIND.
SO DO THE PA

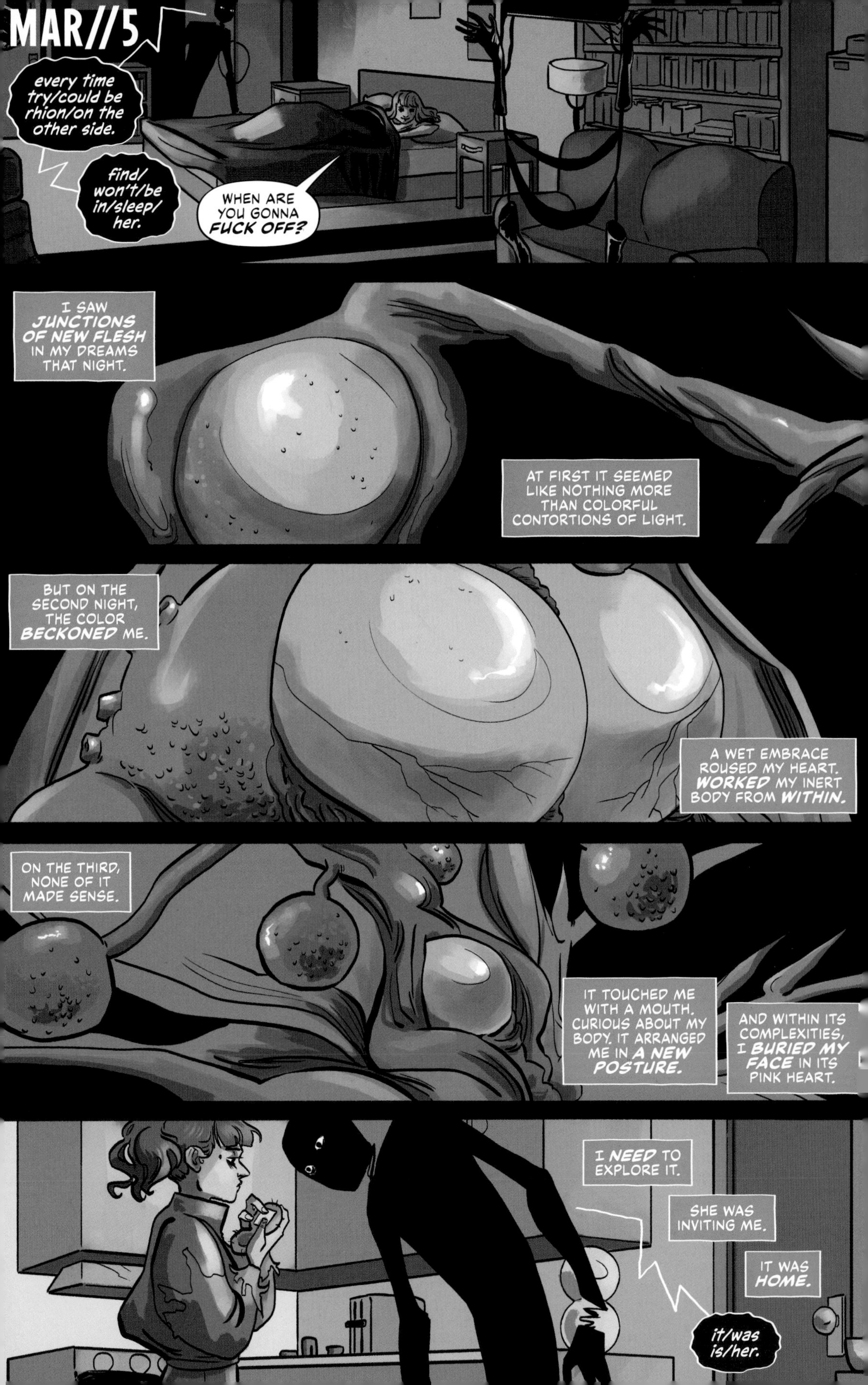
MAR//5
every time try/could be rhion/on the other side.
find/ won't/be in/sleep/ her.
WHEN ARE YOU GONNA FUCK OFF?
I SAW JUNCTIONS OF NEW FLESH IN MY DREAMS THAT NIGHT.
AT FIRST IT SEEMED LIKE NOTHING MORE THAN COLORFUL CONTORTIONS OF LIGHT.
BUT ON THE SECOND NIGHT, THE COLOR BECKONED ME.
A WET EMBRACE ROUSED MY HEART. WORKED MY INERT BODY FROM WITHIN.
ON THE THIRD, NONE OF IT MADE SENSE.
IT TOUCHED ME WITH A MOUTH. CURIOUS ABOUT MY BODY. IT ARRANGED ME IN A NEW POSTURE.
AND WITHIN ITS COMPLEXITIES, I BURIED MY FACE IN ITS PINK HEART.
I NEED TO EXPLORE IT.
SHE WAS INVITING ME.
IT WAS HOME.
it/was is/her.

MAR//11
it is// time to// return.
I CAN FEEL HER BREATH ON MY SKIN. SOFT FLECKS OF MOISTURE AROUSE THE HAIR ON MY NECK. SHE'S SLEEPING RIGHT BESIDE ME.
keep/ descending/ we
become/ until/one.
I'M COMING TO GET YOU. I FEEL YOUR CURIOUS GAZE. RHION.
I can// see her.
she can't//see you.
I LOVE WHAT YOU'VE BECOME, DARLING.
AND I LOVE WHAT YOU'VE MADE ME.
IN THE GREEN, AT THE POINT.
INTO THE UNDER-BRUSH,
I AM THE POINT.
see/you/ her/inside.

THE IMMACULATE FORMS AROUND ME, DEVOUR ME.
THEY DELIBERATELY EXPLORE EVERY ORIFICE THEY CAN FIND. AND I LET THEM.
THIS POTENT FICTION OF DANCING LIMBS BLURS MY REALITY. I KNOW NOTHING BUT THE UNDERBRUSH FOR NOW.
FINGERS RUN ACROSS MY GUMS, TONGUES ACROSS MY THIGHS, HANDS GRIP MY PELVIS.
AND I LET THEM.
DAYS BLUR, OVERLAYING ONE ANOTHER, AS I COME TO COLLECT RHION.
MY PASSIVITY BECOMES MY STRENGTH.
THEY SEE ME.
MY BODY, MY FORM, MY BEING--AN EMBLEMATIC PORTRAIT OF PASSION.
I FEEL SHARPNESS PIERCE MY SPINE. THEY OPEN ME.
AND I LET THEM.
I WANT TO BE DEVOURED.
curious/ bizarre/ exotic.
BEFORE I DEVOUR MYSELF.

APR//7
I ACCUMULATED SCARS AS MOMENTS TURNED TO SPRING.
THE LUSH TEMPERATURE IN THE UNDERBRUSH COOLED WITH MOIST DEW.
AND MY SILVER BODY DANCED IN THE LIGHT, TOWARD HER. YEARNING FOR LOVE.
PAIN BREAKS THE RHYTHM. RECORDING MY POSTURE FOREVER.
BUT THE PLEASURE THAT COMES WITH IT GROWS EMPTY AND STERILE.
JERKING AWAY A WASTE OF TISSUE.
I AM MOIST ENTWINED WITHIN THE GREEN CREEPERS.
WISHING TO COME.
BUT INCREASINGLY AWARE OF THE UNREALITY OF MY BEING.
SCARS, LIKE KNIFE WOUNDS, TO REMIND ME.
I'M SPREAD APART ON STEEL RAILS. METERING COILS DANCE ALONG MY THIGHS. IT LIVES IN MY BODY.
FOR LOVE?

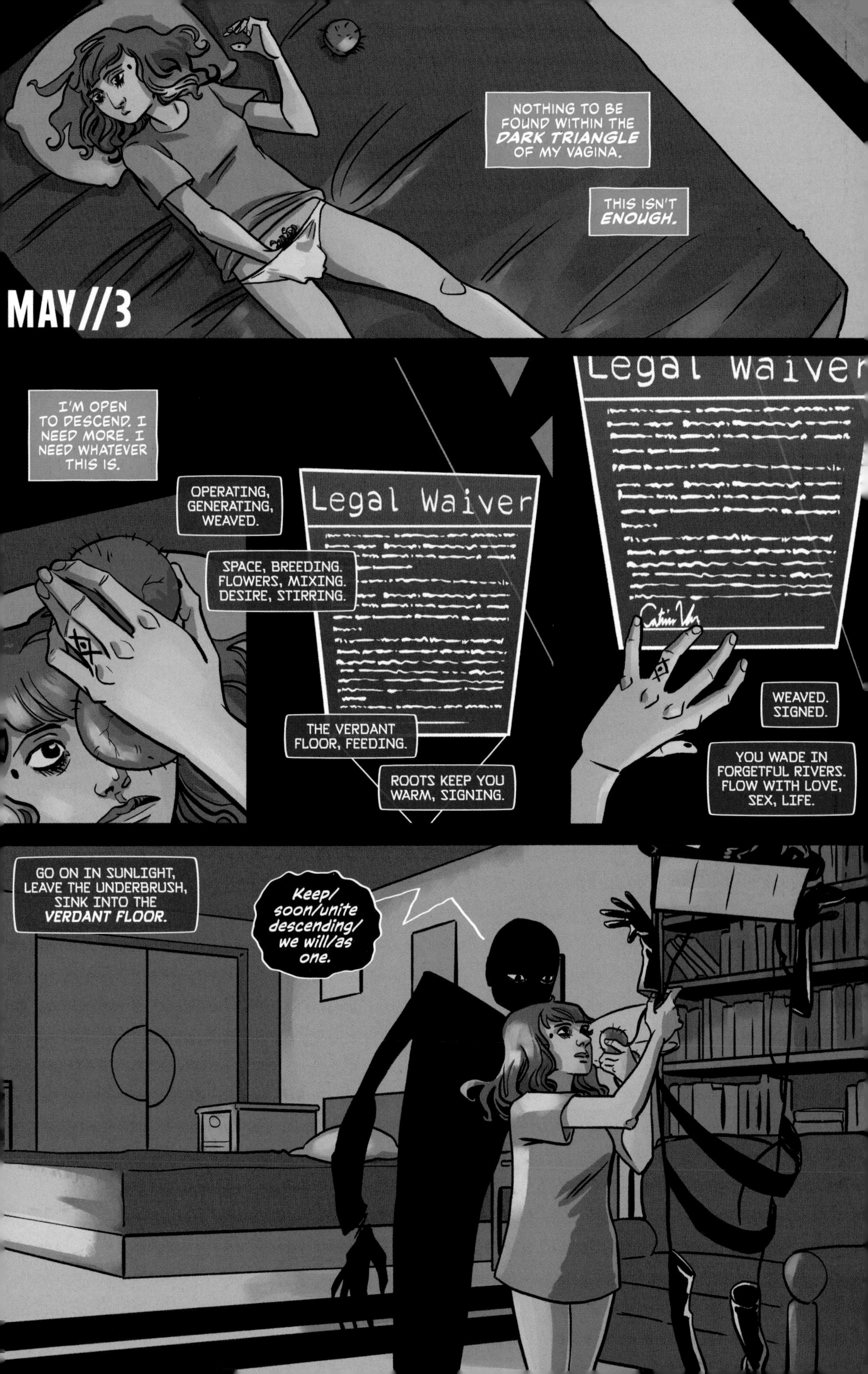
NOTHING TO BE FOUND WITHIN THE DARK TRIANGLE OF MY VAGINA.
THIS ISN'T ENOUGH.
MAY//3
I'M OPEN TO DESCEND. I NEED MORE. I NEED WHATEVER THIS IS.
OPERATING, GENERATING, WEAVED.
SPACE, BREEDING. FLOWERS, MIXING. DESIRE, STIRRING.
Legal Waiver
THE VERDANT FLOOR, FEEDING.
ROOTS KEEP YOU WARM, SIGNING.
Legal Waiver
WEAVED. SIGNED.
YOU WADE IN FORGETFUL RIVERS. FLOW WITH LOVE, SEX, LIFE.
GO ON IN SUNLIGHT, LEAVE THE UNDERBRUSH, SINK INTO THE VERDANT FLOOR.
Keep/ soon/unite descending/ we will/as one.

JULY//7
THERE'S NO FLOWERY VERSE THIS TIME. NO POETIC EDDA TO CAUSE *THIS PLUNGE.*
AND YET, IT ROLLS OVER ME ALL THE SAME.
THE EDGES OF MY FLESH BECOME POROUS WITHIN *THE VERDANT FLOOR.*
BODIES ARE SPLAYED OUT IN COMPLEX GEOMETRIC SHAPES.
WEAVING. JOINING. BECOMING ONE.
AND I CAN'T REMEMBER WHO I USED TO BE.

TOO MANY MINDS IN MY BODY NOW. ARMS PULL AT ME.
POLLUTING MY PLEASURE AS I LONG TO COME.
EDGING, BUT NEVER FINDING LOVE. HER.
SEEKING BLISS, BUT TOILING IN JEALOUSY. SHE'S WITH SOMEONE ELSE.
KNOWING SHE'S JUST, BEYOND, THE NEXT BODY. I CAN FIND HER.
SO, I GIVE IN.

AND I...

FINALLY...

COME.

OCT//5
TIME BLURS\THE MOISTURE EVAPORATES\ TURNING EVERYTHING RICH/MELLOW.
DON'T KNOW/ WHEN I AM\ DON'T CARE.

BEYOND THE HORIZON OF EARTHLY PLEASURE. COMING\AND\COMING.
EVERY ORGASM SKIRTS ME\CLOSER TO THE EDGE\OF MY OWN CONSCIOUSNESS.

I LEARN THINGS\ REMEMBER THINGS\ I NEVER/ONCE KNEW.
I DON'T HAVE\LIPS TO SPEAK\THIS KNOWLEDGE.

IF I DID\ THEN IT WOULD/ FIND ME.
would become/
/not let over/
/the edge.

SO I GIVE MYSELF.

\to/ \my/\self/ \to become/ \reborn/

I BELIEVED/
I WAS/
A WOMAN.

YOU WERE A
RECEIVER. YOU
HAD A LIFE.

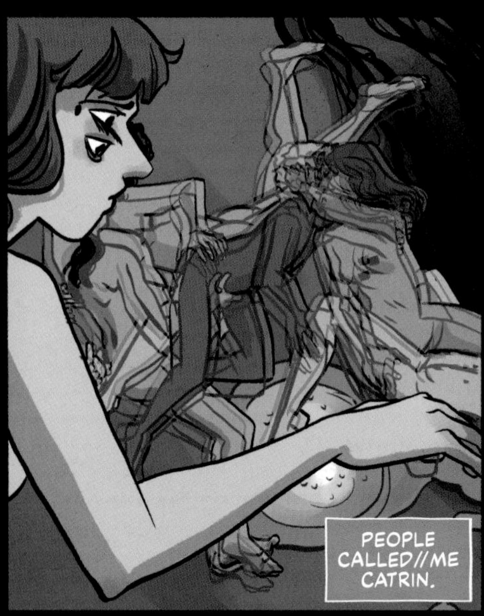
PEOPLE
CALLED//ME
CATRIN.

YOU
SHOULDN'T
BE SO SURE.

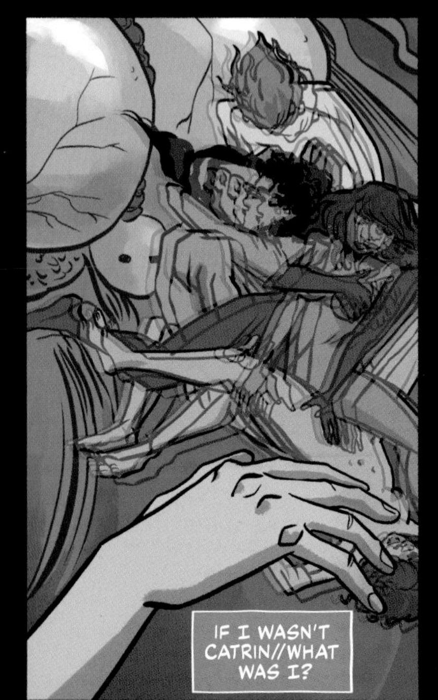
IF I WASN'T
CATRIN//WHAT
WAS I?

WERE
YOU ME?

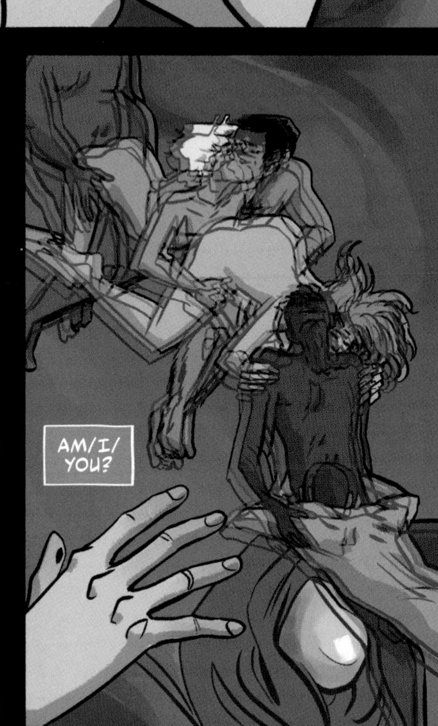
AM/I/
YOU?

IT/DOES NOT/MATTER.
YOU CAN'T BARE IT/I CAN'T BARE IT/YOU CAN'T BARE IT.

YOU WERE/ ARE ONE RECEIVER/ PERSON.

NOW YOU/ARE TWO
ALONE/ TOGETHER.

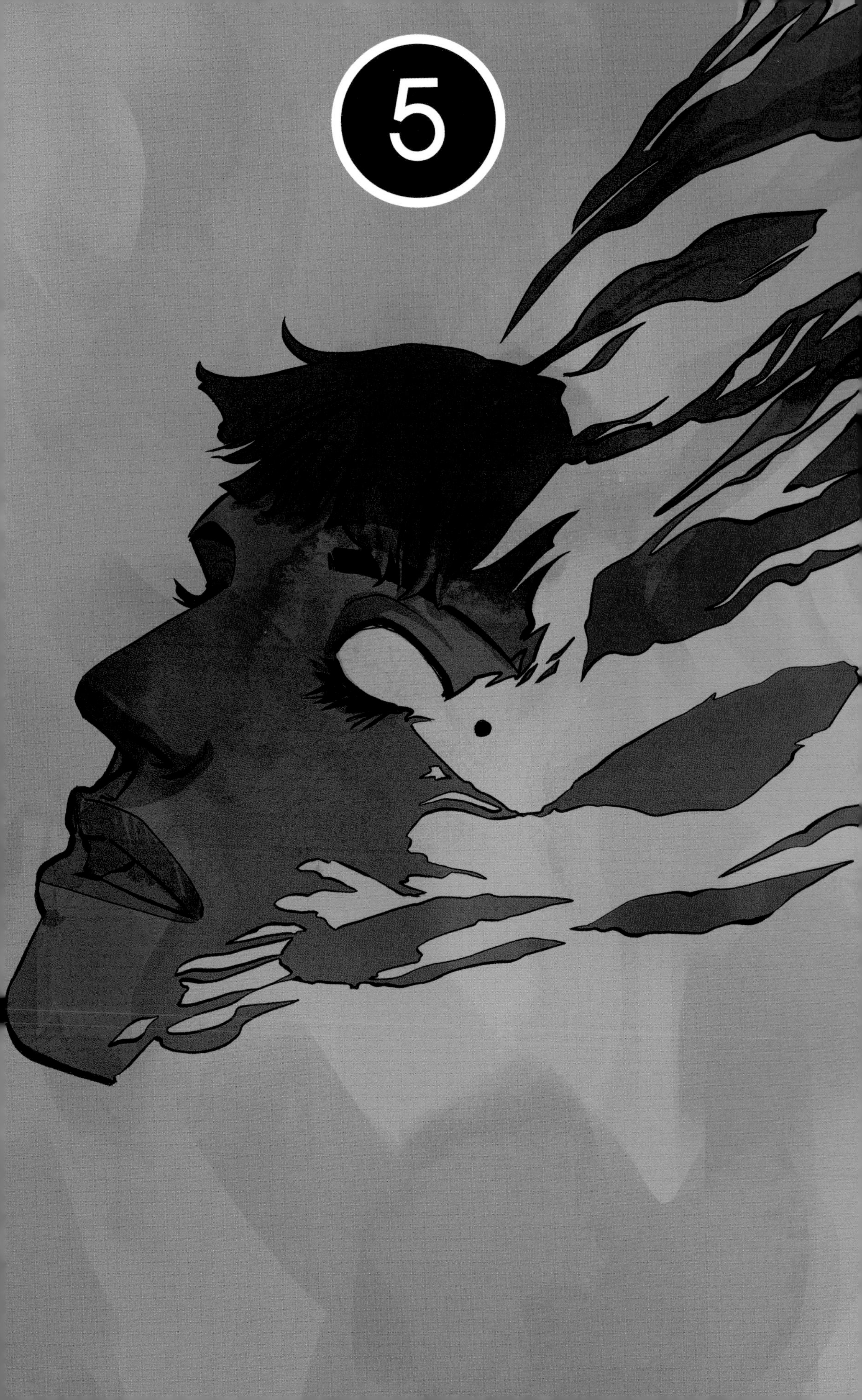
5

A LIFE

WEAVE THE WIND. I HAVE NO GHOSTS

Now you / see what you used to be / itself
You love and change when moving wildly toward darkness.
Enter the Leviathan / as it too / enters you
Now see / you spend a life finding / yourself.

ELSE//WHEN
YOU'RE THE ONE WHO RUINED IT. YOU LET HER HIT YOU.
ALL THAT PAIN AND YOU DON'T EVEN REMEMBER HER FACE.
YOU CAN'T. A PATTERN?
ALL YOU REMEMBER IS THE BACK OF HER HAND.
OR WAS IT YOUR NAILS CUTTING INTO THE SOFT TISSUE OF HER FLESH?
HER GHOST LINGERS WITH YOU.
THEY ALL DO.

SPARKLING LIKE A RIBBON, WRAPPED AROUND THE GLOW OF THE CITY, YOU HAD A PARTY. YOU LIED TO YOUR FRIENDS.
THEIR NAMES? THEY DON'T MATTER, THEY'RE INTERCHANGEABLE.
YOU WANTED TO BE SOMETHING OTHER THAN WHAT YOU WERE. IT SHOULD HAVE BEEN VALIDATING. THEIR TELLING SILENCE MADE YOU INHUMAN.
THAT WAS A CHOICE. NOW IT'S A PROBLEM FOR BOTH OF US.
YOU HALF REMEMBER EVERYTHING YOU WANT TO FORGET.
MOST THINGS WILL NEVER HAPPEN. THIS WILL.
YOU MADE SURE NO ONE SAW YOU FOR WHAT YOU REALLY WERE.
YOU LIED TO YOURSELF, KNOWING YOU'D REPLACE YOUR LIFE SOON ENOUGH.
THEY'VE FORGOTTEN WHAT YOU SAID, BUT NOT HOW YOU MADE THEM FEEL.
SOMETHING LIKE THIS CANNOT BE HIDDEN.
IT CAN ONLY BE DENIED.
THE LIFE YOU ONCE HAD IS GONE.
THE CHOICE YOU FACE NOW IS ABOUT THE LIFE YOU HAVE NEXT.

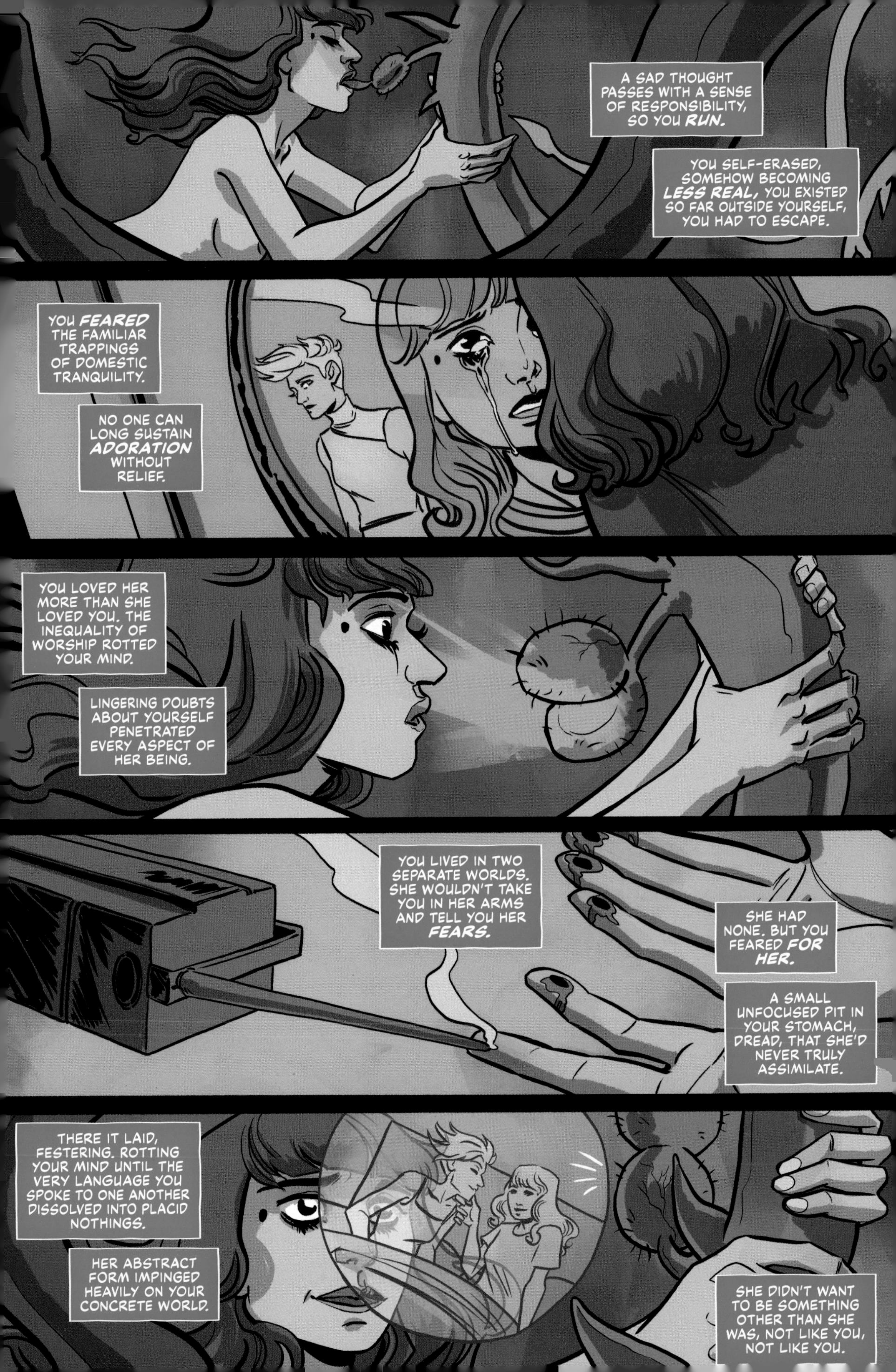

A SAD THOUGHT PASSES WITH A SENSE OF RESPONSIBILITY, SO YOU RUN.
YOU SELF-ERASED, SOMEHOW BECOMING LESS REAL, YOU EXISTED SO FAR OUTSIDE YOURSELF, YOU HAD TO ESCAPE.
YOU FEARED THE FAMILIAR TRAPPINGS OF DOMESTIC TRANQUILITY.
NO ONE CAN LONG SUSTAIN ADORATION WITHOUT RELIEF.
YOU LOVED HER MORE THAN SHE LOVED YOU. THE INEQUALITY OF WORSHIP ROTTED YOUR MIND.
LINGERING DOUBTS ABOUT YOURSELF PENETRATED EVERY ASPECT OF HER BEING.
YOU LIVED IN TWO SEPARATE WORLDS. SHE WOULDN'T TAKE YOU IN HER ARMS AND TELL YOU HER FEARS.
SHE HAD NONE. BUT YOU FEARED FOR HER.
A SMALL UNFOCUSED PIT IN YOUR STOMACH, DREAD, THAT SHE'D NEVER TRULY ASSIMILATE.
THERE IT LAID, FESTERING. ROTTING YOUR MIND UNTIL THE VERY LANGUAGE YOU SPOKE TO ONE ANOTHER DISSOLVED INTO PLACID NOTHINGS.
HER ABSTRACT FORM IMPINGED HEAVILY ON YOUR CONCRETE WORLD.
SHE DIDN'T WANT TO BE SOMETHING OTHER THAN SHE WAS, NOT LIKE YOU, NOT LIKE YOU.

REMEMBER, THAT NO ONE IS LOVE.
YOU CHOSE THIS, BEFORE YOU WERE READY, YOU WANTED IT.
TO BE MADE.
THEY HAD QUESTIONS ABOUT HER.
YOU GAVE YOUR FLESH TO THE MACHINE.
YOU DIDN'T WANT HER// THEM TO KNOW THE TRUTH.
BECAUSE YOU FEAR YOURSELF.
REMADE IN SOMEONE ELSE'S EYE.
THE BEING LOOMING IN THE MIRROR/NO NOT THAT/THE ONE LOOKING BACK AT YOU, IS MORE THAN A REFLECTION.
YOU DIDN'T LIKE WHAT YOU SAW. SO YOU LIED. YOU INVENTED REALITY.

YOU WERE TOO MUCH.
YOU ACTED TRANSPARENT BUT HID EVERYTHING.
THEY HAD QUESTIONS, YOU REFUSED ANSWERS, EVENTUALLY THEY LEFT.
BECAUSE THEY SAW YOU FOR WHAT YOU WERE.
YOU TOLD ME THIS. YOU TOLD ME EVERYTHING.
AND IT CUTS YOU LIKE A BLADE.
HOW MANY PEOPLE HAVE YOU KILLED?
HOW MANY OF THEM WERE YOU?

YOU DON'T KNOW WHAT YOU ARE ANYMORE. BUT YOU ARE A PERSON. MAKING CHOICES.
FOLLOWING A PATH YOU CAN'T SEE.
YOU ARE POWERFUL. IMMACULATE. COMPLEX.
YOU CHOOSE THE WORDS I SPEAK NOW.
YOU'VE SPOKEN THESE WORDS BEFORE. MANY TIMES. YOU'VE LIVED THESE MOMENTS IN ROTATION.
ALWAYS PRESENT IN A MILLION PLACES, MOVING TOWARD A MILLION MORE.
BUT THE SENSE THAT YOU WERE PARTICIPATING WAS ONLY EVER AN ILLUSION.
WHEN YOU WAKE UP YOU'LL UNDERSTAND.

THE VOICE YOU HEAR IN YOUR HEAD IS *YOURS.*
BUT THE WORDS BELONG TO *ANOTHER.*
NO SIGNAL
UNKNOWN RECEIVER
BZZT BZZT

HEH... HELLO?

GOODBYE, CATRIN.
IT'S ME. IT'S RHION.

I'M SORRY. I JUST--
SHH. DOESN'T MATTER NOW.
YOU CAN'T SEE ME. STOP TRYING.

PLEASE. WHERE ARE YOU?
I DON'T KNOW. DOESN'T MATTER.
WE'RE FINALLY EQUAL NOW. THIS WILL BECOME FAMILIAR TO YOU IF YOU LET IT. WHAT YOU'RE FEELING INSIDE CAN BE MADE TRANQUIL.
EMBRACE YOURSELF.

WHEREVER I AM, I WON'T BE BACK. BUT I LOVE YOU.
LAY DOWN. LISTEN TO ME.

I'LL TELL YOU WHAT I KNOW.

YOU ARE NOTHING.

JUST LIKE ME.

YOURS. LIKE A KISS FROM A CREATURE IN THE CORNER OF YOUR EYE. ALWAYS.

A BEACON, BECKONING TRANSMISSIONS FROM YOUR FLESH, LIKE LIGHT IN THE DARK.

YOU ARE BEAUTIFUL, INFINITE, AND LIVING WITHIN THE BELLY OF YOUR HAND.

YOU GET IT. IT'S A PERFECT CIRCLE. ELEGANT. BEAUTIFUL.

IT'S YOU. YOU LOVE IT. YOUR HEART POUNDS IN YOUR CHEST.

JUST LIKE ME.

YOU ARE EVERYTHING.

IT'S BEEN A PLEASURE TALKING TO YOU.

LOOK YOURSELF IN THE EYE.
YOU. WERE. ALWAYS. TWO.
IN EACH MOMENT YOU SPENT WITH THEM, YOU SHROUDED YOURSELF IN MIST.
ALWAYS PREFERRING SYMMETRICAL PARALLELS OF FLESH. FILLING THE SPACES IN YOURSELF WITH OTHERS.

HOLD STILL, BABE.
DOUBT. YOU KNOW IT WELL.
WONDERING IF IT'S A HOLOGRAM OF YOURSELF STARING BACK AT YOU.

AS ONE STARED INTO THE MIRROR, TWO ALWAYS STARED BACK.
THESE ARE THE SENTENCES AND MEMORIES YOU TELL YOURSELF, LINGERING LIKE GHOSTS.

YOU WERE TOO YOUNG, THEN. FEAR LEFT TERRIBLE SCARS ON YOUR EYES.
THOSE CONTORTED FEATURES. THE SPASTIC LURCH.

HERE IS ONE YOU LONGED TO FORGET. JUST LIKE HER FACE. IT'S NOT THAT SIMPLE.

IT NEVER IS. YOU'RE STUCK ON A CYCLE. DO YOU FEEL THAT?

THE THING YOU CAN'T AVOID IS YOURSELF.
YOU GIVE IN, OVER AND OVER, TO THE KILLING SADNESS.

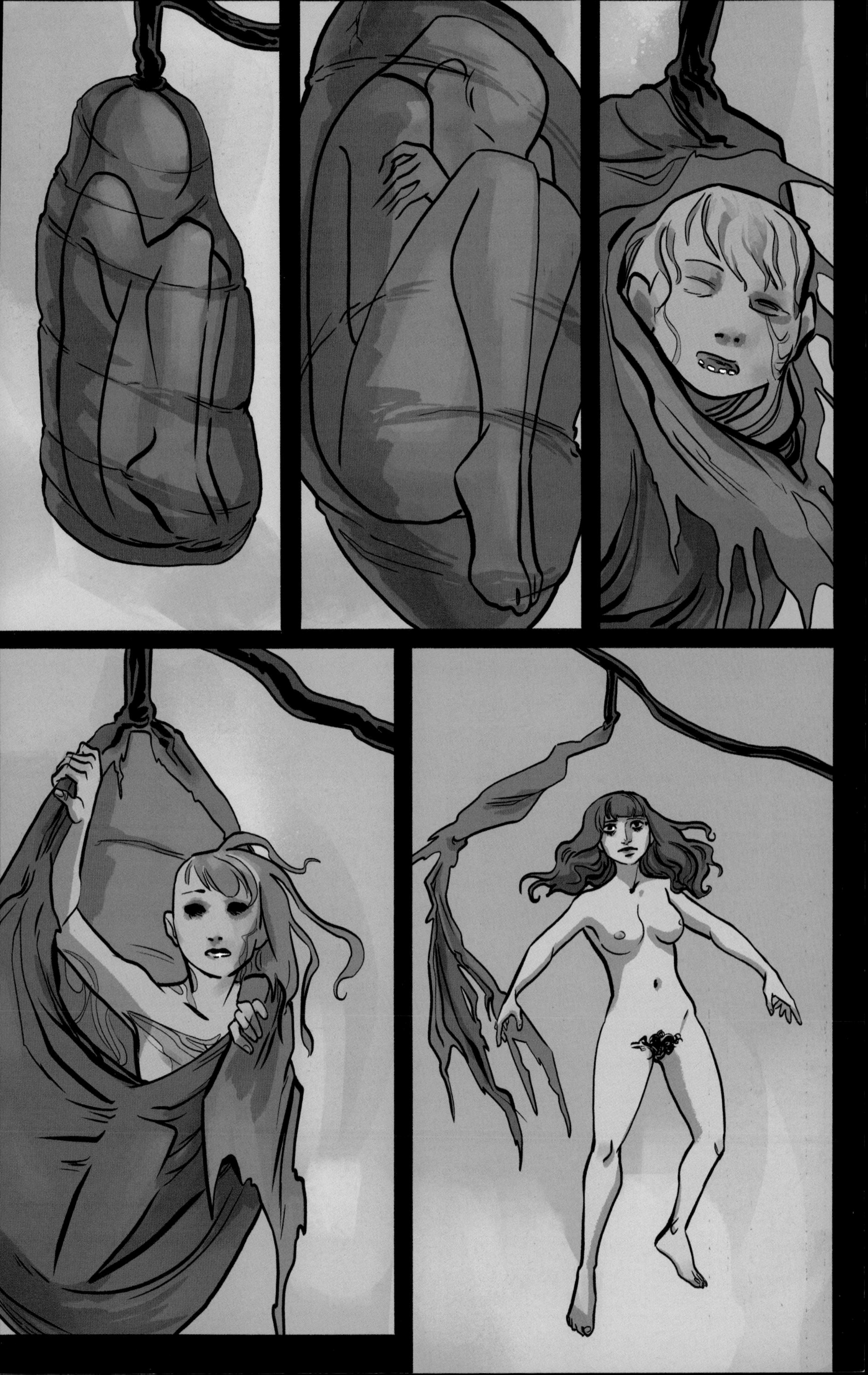

IT'S COMPLEX. THE SILENCE YOU OBSERVE WOULD BE RUDE IF YOU WERE HUMAN, BUT YOU'RE NOT HUMAN. YOU'RE A *STORY.*
NOW YOU FINALLY SEE. SEE YOURSELF FOR WHAT YOU ARE.

WHAT YOU CONTINUALLY BECOME. A NEW PERSON.

BUT YOUR PAIN MAKES YOU REAL TO YOURSELF.

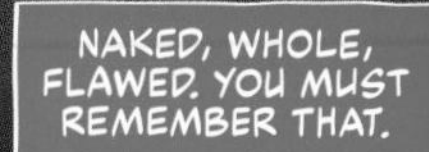
NAKED, WHOLE, FLAWED. YOU MUST REMEMBER THAT.

HOW DO YOU FEEL ABOUT YOUR CREATOR?

YOU EXISTED SO FAR INTO ABSTRACTION, IN ISOLATION, THAT IN ORDER TO BECOME REAL AGAIN YOU HAD TO ESCAPE.
HOW DO YOU FEEL ABOUT YOURSELF?
YOU ARE CAPABLE OF MONITORING YOUR OWN STATE OF MIND.
AREN'T YOU?
STOP LIVING SOMEONE ELSE'S LIFE.
WE ALL LOVE ONE *ANOTHER* HERE/*WEAVED*/WE ARE *ALL* CONNECTED NOW.
YOU HANG THERE SHUDDERING/YOUR BODY IN RUIN/GREAT HOLES PUNCHED IN YOUR SIDES/LIKE A *MONSTER.*
THAT *OTHER* //CREATURE// IS NOT YOU.
GRAAH!

I'VE GIVEN YOU A CONNECTION.
YOU NEED NOT LONG FOR MORE.
FUCK YOU. I'M DONE RUNNING.
YOU ARE DREAMING IN A WORLD THAT IS NOT YOURS.
I MADE YOU A RECEIVER. I WILL NEVER REJECT YOU.
I DON'T CARE. LET ME GO.
I DON'T NEED YOU ANYMORE.
BUT, CATRIN... I AM Y--
SHUNK
AAH!

FUCK!

THE FUCK IS GOING ON?
GET UP. KEEP MOVING.
EVERYTHING WITHIN YOU, YOU'VE GIVEN TO ME.

YOU LOVE ME. WE'RE INSEPARABLE
NOT LISTENING.

YOU'RE NOW ***WEAVED*** TO ***EVERYONE.***
KILL IT.

I WEAVED ***YOU*** TO EVERYONE.
WE ALL LOVE YOU.

PLEASE. NO. WE ALL LOVE YOU.
WE ALL--

THIS IS THE LAST STORY I TELL ABOUT MYSELF.
ALL OF IT, REMINDING ME, I DON'T JUST BELONG *HERE.* I BELONG *EVERYWHERE.*
LEAVE THIS ISLAND OF SOLITUDE.
SO I DECIDE ONCE MORE TO SPIN OUT OF SIGHT.
INTO THE ARMS OF ANOTHER. THIS TIME, A *FAMILIAR* FACE.
THE ANSWER. *HER.* OF COURSE IT'S *HER.*
IT'S *ALWAYS BEEN* HER.
SHE STANDS THERE, RADIANT. COMMANDING. BLEEDING LIGHT...
...WITH SLOW, METICULOUS GRACE I UNRAVEL BEFORE HER...

...AND IN OUR UNION, SPREAD OUT ACROSS THE SKY, FOR THE FIRST TIME, I SEE MYSELF.
/FINALLY WHOLE/.
A NEW BEGINNING//THE END

Issue 1
ELIZABETH TORQUE
Incentive Cover

Issue 2
LEILA LEIZ
Incentive Cove

Lonely Receiver™

JEN HICKMAN
sketchbook

In a book like LONELY RECEIVER, where loud, unreal color dominates so much of the book, it's important to think about design primarily in terms of silhouette/shape language: Can I tell who this person is even if all the colors are batshit?

LONELY RECEIVER has a small cast, so ensuring that they all read different from each other wasn't too much of a headache.

The color palettes I used for various times of day ended up having a life of their own—the late night pink-and-blue started to feel like code for emotional extremes, the orange and teal of dawn starting feeling like anticipation (then dread), and so on.

I also tried to push the idea of using unreal color schemes for high drama, then bringing in more local palettes for establishing "normalcy."

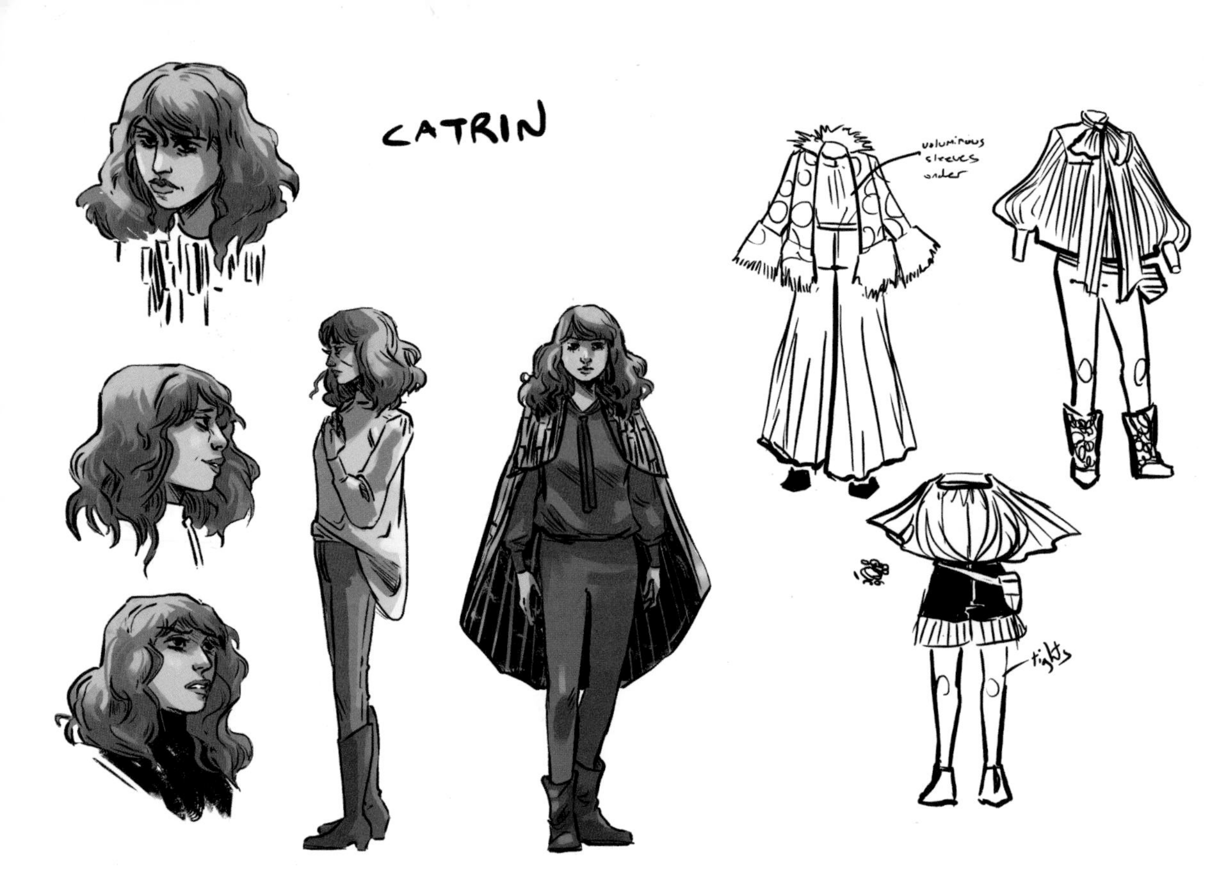

Zac noted that Catrin is 38, and referenced Natasha Lyonne for her inspiration. I wanted to keep an unpleasant balance between Catrin's age and her styling choices—everything should feel a little young on her, in addition to being very loud and high-fashion.

Catrin's fashion choices, at all moments, were meant to hide the actual shape of her body (Zac's brilliant idea), which I thought was a lovely tension with how much time she spent in the book naked.

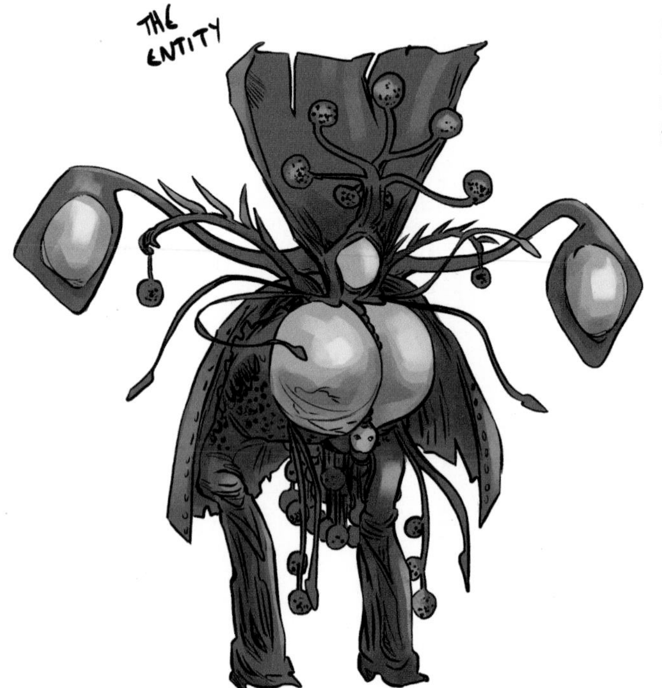

I tried to mash together every Beksiński painting with hyper-realized genitalia/things that felt like genitals.

Making Rhion and Hazel look very much alike while still being definitely two different people was a challenge! Fashion helped, and then in the comic itself, body language sealed the deal.

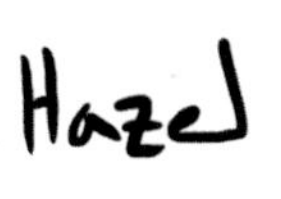

ABOUT THE CREATORS OF

Lonely Receiver™

ZAC THOMPSON

@ZacBeThompson ZacBeThompson

Zac Thompson is a critically acclaimed writer from Prince Edward Island, Canada. He's written titles like *Marvelous X-Men, Cable,* and *Yondu* for Marvel Comics. Along with indie books such as UNDONE BY BLOOD, *No One's Rose,* and *The Dregs.* His original graphic novella, THE REPLACER, was called the best horror comic of 2019 by HorrorDNA. His debut novel, *Weaponized,* was the winner of the 2016 CryptTV horror fiction contest. Zac is an avid cyclist and overly excitable weirdo.

JEN HICKMAN

@thejensington thejensington

Jen Hickman is a visual storyteller and a graduate of the Savannah College of Art and Design's Sequential Art Program. Their primary passions are exciting narratives, good coffee and exceptional grammar.

SIMON BOWLAND

@SimonBowland SimonBowlandLettering

Simon has been lettering comics for over a decade and is currently working for DC, Image, Valiant, Dark Horse, Dynamite, 2000AD and IDW, amongst others. His debut AfterShock project was UNHOLY GRAIL. Born and bred in England, Simon still lives there today alongside his wife and their tabby cat.

MORE FROM THESE CREATORS

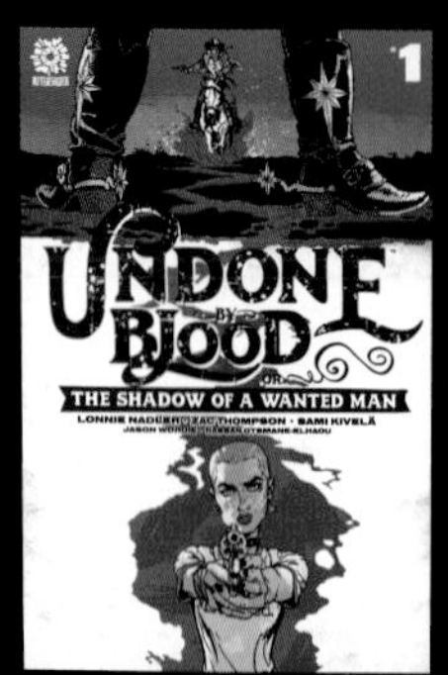

Lonnie Nadler / Zac Thompson
Sami Kivelä / Jason Wordie
Hassan Otsmane-Elhaou

Zac Thompson / Arjuna Susini
Dee Cunniffe / Marshall Dillon

Zac Thompson / Andy Clarke
Dalibor Talajic / Dan Brown
Charles Pritchett

Ted Anderson / Jen Hickman
Marshall Dillon